IT FEELS LIKE
HOME

CLARE LUKAS

K bear
thanks for being
friends with us assholes
for so long ♡
ali

It Feels Like Home

Editor: BLM Editing Services | Bri Lind
Cover Designer: Creative Paramita
Formatting: Good Girl Author Services | Kalie Gerwig

For permission to reproduce any of this novel, please contact Clare Lukas
at authorclarelukas@gmail.com

For information on sales of this book, go to
https://authorclarelukas.com/

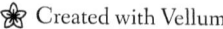 Created with Vellum

blurb

Jacelyn Waverly might need a twelve-step program for jerks.

One jerk, in particular, Ky Linley, because even two years apart hasn't stopped the butterflies from taking flight in her stomach when he's around.

After humiliating her in her freshman year and starting rumors that dogged her reputation, Ky shouldn't get a second chance. Still, she's returned home older and wiser, and everyone seems different now. But with an angry sister, an overworked mom, a father on the opposite side of the country, and a best friend who is just starting to fall in love for the first time, it all seems like a lot.

But sometimes, growing up feels like coming home.

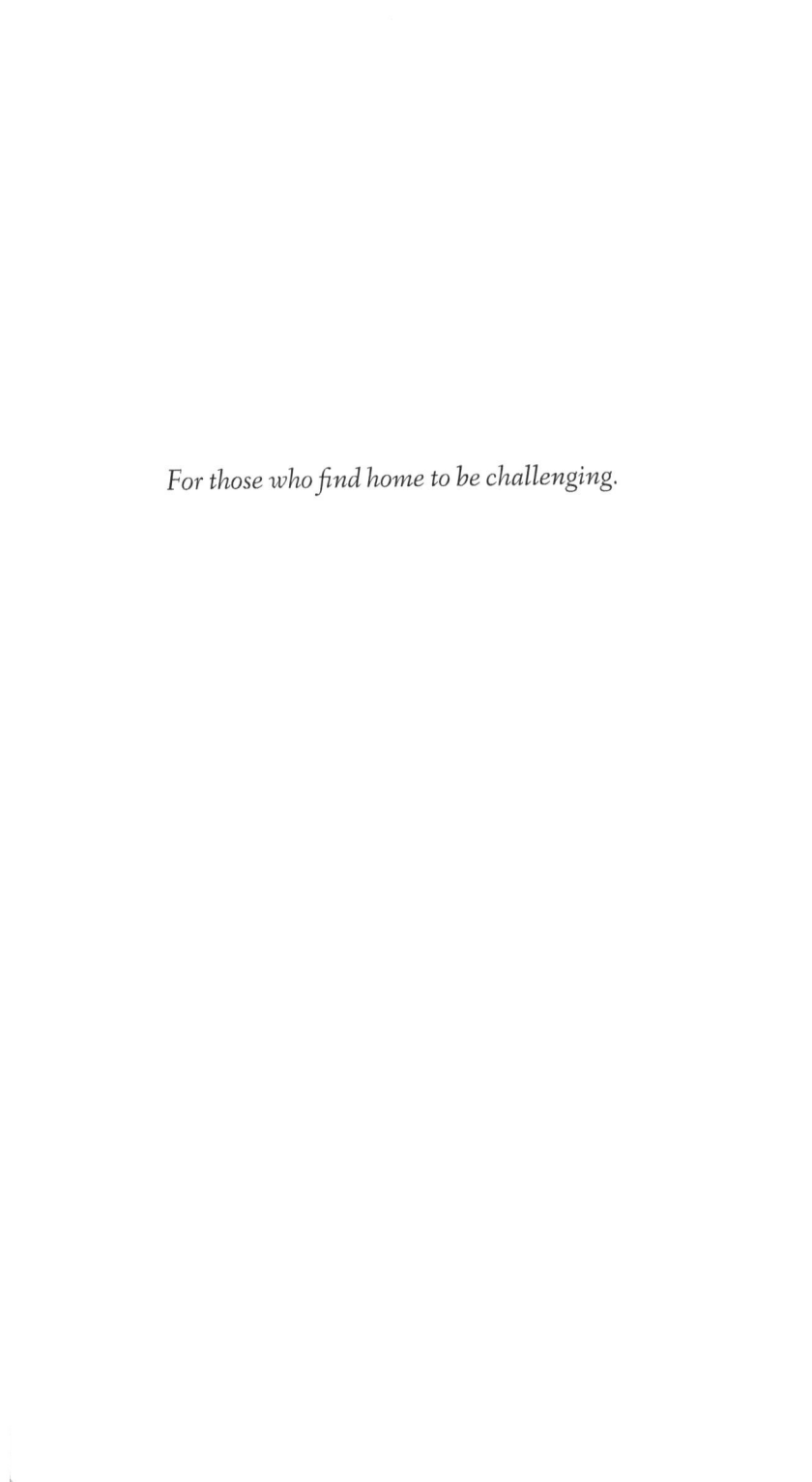

For those who find home to be challenging.

playlist

- All Of Me – Sofia Karlberg
- Worms – Ashnikko
- Booty (feat. Latto) – Saucy Santana, Latto
- Oh my god – G(I-DLE)
- Never Felt So Alone – Labrinth
- Slow (feat. Ciara) – Jackson Wang, Ciara
- Believe – Cher
- Shoop – Salt-N-Pepa
- Wish You Were Here – Pink Floyd
- Bad Life – Sigrid, Bring Me The Horizon
- Where Is My Mind? – Tkay Maidza
- Loser – Sueco
- Shoong! (feat. LISA of BLACKPINK) – Taeyang, Lisa
- If We Ever Broke Up – Mae Stephens
- Whoomp! (There It Is) – Tag Team
- Surrender – Cheap Trick
- Meet Me At Our Spot – THE ANXIETY, WILLOW, Tyler Cole
- Sunshower – EPEX

- It's Called: Freefall – Paris Paloma
- They Don't Love It – Jack Harlow
- Work It – Missy Elliot
- Maroon –Taylor Swift
- I Lived – OneRepublic

contents

one

. . .

Two years ago

"I SAW YOU LAST NIGHT. During the last dance, you were kissing that hot as a cayenne pepper, Ky Linley," my best friend Peter said, as he shook his finger and head at me. With an over-dramatic sigh, he tsked and gave me a look that was singularly judgemental. I had met this boy in fourth grade, and he knew me better than anyone. He knew that my kiss with Ky was my first kiss, and his act of disapproval sat uncomfortably on my heart. I couldn't help the color that flooded my cheeks as I looked down and examined my veggie dog.

"I'm joking!" Peter pushed my shoulder and nearly shoved me over. "Spill the tea!"

A smile played at my lips as I remembered the incredible moment when Ky tilted my chin up and first pressed his lips to mine. "All Of Me" by Sofia Karlberg was playing and the room was dark and the lights were twinkling. He smelt like Eros by Versace; such an expensive cologne for a sixteen year old guy.

I sighed, dreamily.

A sharp thwap to my knee brought me out of my reverie. "Details, Jacelyn!"

I sucked on my lips to keep my smile at bay. Peter and my sister Maris were aware that my crush on Ky was life-long. I had been googly-eyed over him since my sister had first invited him to a birthday party when she was in first grade.

"Well, I didn't kiss *him*. He kissed *me*," I clarified.

Peter made a face and nodded. "Right. Looks like you were fighting him off when I was watching."

I swatted at him. "Of course not! That's not what I mean, and you know it!"

Peter laughed. "Well, that is one thing to tick off your bucket list. Should we bronze your lips?"

"I don't have a bucket list, I'm fifteen, stupid. It was just a kiss." I huffed and tried to play it off. I really couldn't pull it off though since a deranged grin quickly stole over my lips. I'd been feeling more and more like I'd gone mental since last night anyway. Why not show proof?

"Maybe you need a bucket list. Your phone just vibrated. Since I'm here, who could that possibly be? Mr. Hot Lips himself?" Peter sucked in his cheeks and opened his eyes wide. He looked demented.

Ky wasn't just my forever-crush, he was the *it* guy–super popular, athletic and beautiful; he was expected to go far in life. I wasn't likely to ever graduate to those ranks of high school success. Not that any of that made Ky Linley more special in my eyes. I had been in love with him before that. I fell in love with him when he stole a cupcake from me when I was only five. It took ten years for him to notice me.

My phone vibrated again. Peter and I grabbed for it at the same time, and I beat him to it by a hair. Picking it up, I read it and couldn't help but laugh out loud. Ky had been all flattery the last few weeks. He might have kissed me only last night, but he'd been flirty for a while now. Maris hated it. My older sister was suspicious about how much attention he was giving me.

"What?" Peter grabbed for my phone and wrestled it from my fist. He read it, and his eyebrows raised. "What the hell?"

"He's been telling me he thinks I'm sexy. Beautiful even. I know not to believe him, Peter. I know I'm just plain o' Jacelyn Waverly with the same body I've had since the sixth grade. I'm short, skinny and have no boobs. I even lack any discernible waist or booty. For all intents and purposes, I'm shaped like a ten year old boy. Still, it's nice to be told you're pretty. You know? It's nice to hear good things, even if the person saying it doesn't mean it."

I bit my lip and glanced down at my hands. Being a fifteen year old girl sucked.

Peter frowned, holding up my phone. "Really though? This is the kind of stuff he says to you? This is messed up."

I rolled my eyes. "He's just being funny. He isn't serious. Don't be so judgy."

"No. No. Listen to me." Peter sighed. "I totally see why you would get excited about him noticing you finally. If he noticed me, I would probably get excited, and I am not crushing on him. But he talks to you in a trashy way that pisses me off. It's disrespectful and not okay." He tossed the phone back my way.

I pouted and looked down at the newest text. "Your

Korean upbringing is showing through. Stop being so conservative. He is just flattering me."

"No." He choked out a laugh. "He's asking you for a naked picture of your ta-tas, Jace. I'm not being a prude. I think it's a real jackass thing to request. Not to mention illegal. If you send it, it's a felony for distributing child pornography."

I aimed the phone at him. "Not fair. If he asked you for a picture of your chest, you wouldn't be saying that."

Peter had been out of the closet since the beginning of ninth grade. His very traditional Korean family was firmly in denial of what they considered his 'American' ways. Still, Peter didn't let it get him down. He openly lived the life he wanted to live, even though he took a lot of flack for it at school. We didn't live in the most accepting town. It was small, and people were afraid of things that were different, and being Korean in a predominantly white Anglo-Saxon area was different enough, without adding homosexual on top of it. I had a lot of respect for him and the choices he made and how he never folded.

"Nuh-uh, sister. Asking to see my boobs and asking to see your boobs, are two totally different things. You have to know that. One is outlandish, the other is just not cool." Peter pulled out his own phone and checked the time.

I inhaled trying to be patient but rolled my eyes at the ridiculousness of the conversation. Peter was overreacting. It was flirting. All older guys did it. I would never send them, and Ky knew that. Still I texted back, playing along.

> Me: I'm too shy. Send me a pic of your chest and I'll consider it.

> DreamKy: I see how it is. You're trying to objectify me. How bout a picture of you in your bra, nothing showing?

> Me: LOL!!! I don't think so!

Peter read over my shoulder and made a sound of disgust. "I'm happy to see you find that funny," he said in disappointment. I didn't enjoy seeing that look on his face. I wasn't ready for him to burst my bubble yet though.

I rocked from side to side and hummed trying to think of something mature and coy to say back to this older boy who was suddenly into me. I glanced at Peter and shook my head. "Just let it go!"

"Whatever! You're going to only make it worse by playing it up with him. Soon, you two will be sexting."

I gave my friend a 'get real' look. "I'm fifteen. I'm not experienced enough to know how to sext."

He shrugged and said, "Guys like him are all the same—pretty, yet vile. But you do you, boo!"

I exhaled frustrated with all the hate that Peter was laying out. "I'm going to do just that. You're wrong about him. He's just playing around. He likes me, and this is just how he shows it." I pierced him with a look.

Peter shook his head, waved his hand at me dismissively like he was done with me, and the subject was closed. He stood from where he sat next to me on the floor and made a beeline for my computer on my desk. I had a girly desk. It was white with gold filigree, and Peter would look ridiculous there, if it weren't for the fact that he was wearing lavender shorts and had on a mint green golf shirt.

Without waiting for my permission, he opened it up

and started searching for the latest Korean pop music news. He is a first generation Korean-American, and his family traveled back to South Korea yearly to visit family. He easily read the Korean language and the K-Pop news sources from their news sites.

I sighed. I hated fighting with him, and this was a dumb thing to fight over. He knew how much I loved Ky. I didn't know why he was suddenly raining on my parade, when he should've been happy for me.

I decided to ignore Peter since he wanted to ignore me and went back to texting Ky until I saw my friend's shoulder relaxing.

"I have to go soon, Jace. I don't want to go with us fighting. I'm sorry for making you feel like I'm mad at you. I'm not. I just want more for you than a guy who only values you for your body." He gestured to my phone with his chin.

I nodded and smiled at his olive branch. "I'm sorry too. I should be more appreciative of the fact that you care. But I want you to know, I am happy. I want you to be happy for me."

Peter didn't look particularly happy, but he tried to give me a weak smile of support. "Tomorrow is Sunday; church and then family dinner. I wish I could escape."

Every Sunday the Kim's spend time together. They did this ritual without deviation. His extended family came over: aunties, uncles, cousins and often friends of the family who were traveling in the area.

I had gone a few times, but the formality made me uncomfortable. His mom was very controlling, and if he suggested doing anything else, it was met with cool disdain and a sharp word of dissent. She would then never let it go. She would bring it up over and over again, making his guilt trips the things of legend.

"What is on the menu this week?" I asked.

"Japchae and contempt. My mother has made me promise not to tell my aunties and uncles about my interest in other boys. She thinks it dishonors my family. They keep telling me I'm not old enough to date anyway." I watched him close my laptop and bit my tongue. We were both too young to date in my dad's opinion too.

He stood. "See you Monday morning?"

"Yep. I'll meet you by your locker?" I stood as he pulled on his shoes. He wore these multicolored Covernat sneakers that cost three times the price of my Keds. I watched him tie them bunny ear style.

His style haircut required tons of product and wouldn't move in a freaking hurricane. Peter was very good looking. He hated his nose and constantly went on about wanting surgery because he thought it was too wide, but I thought it fit his face. His eyes were a dark brown that was warm and thoughtful, and his lips quirked into an engaging smile that was charming and showed off the most adorable dimple on the right side.

My friend was a catch.

He stood upright and stretched before heading to my bedroom door.

"No! We are not leaving it without a hug, Mr. Make-Amends." I shook my head at him, and he smiled and gave me a nod. I tossed my phone down as it vibrated again and stuck my arms out making airplane noises as I raced his way. "Peter Kim, you are a good friend." I squeezed him tightly.

"I know. I know." He leaned back and booped me on the nose. "See ya Monday, Jace."

As soon as my door closed, I leaned against it and stared at my phone. I considered his concerns. I could admit, I was in over my head with a guy asking for things no fifteen year old girl without a chest could satisfy him with. But still, I finally had his attention. It was unlikely to last. I was going to enjoy my fifteen minutes while I had it.

I grabbed my phone and laid down on my back on my bed, head at the foot of the bed, feet on the headboard. I couldn't wait to see him on Monday, but until then I had this.

Me: Peter just left. I can talk to you uninterrupted now.

DreamKy: You couldn't send me nudes because your friend was there, but now you can... I get it.

Me: Goofball. I couldn't send nudes because I don't have the body that would impress you.

DreamKy: How can you say that? Your body was pressed up against me last night and I had a major hard on. I want to see it now.

Maris came down the hall towards my locker at a good speed. She was weaving in and out between people like a woman on a mission, and storm clouds were gathering in her eyes. I could tell she was making a straight line for me, and I smiled a greeting.

My sister was the pretty one in the family, she looked like my mom with her long blonde hair and hazel eyes. I looked like our grandmother with strawberry blonde hair that was too brassy and hazel eyes that leaned toward brown. I was a cliché, whereas my sister was a classic beauty.

She was also in the same grade as Ky. They were both sophomores, while I was just a freshman. My sister wasn't necessarily a part of the 'In Crowd', but she had a large amount of friends where she was active and well liked.

Apparently, she was also irate.

Grabbing my arm, she closed my locker then started pulling me away from the direction of my homeroom. "Mare, I need to go meet Peter and go to class."

She nodded, stopping in her tracks and changed directions walking in the opposite way. "That is a great idea. Let's go find Peter!"

I followed her shining, golden head as she ignored people calling her name or those wishing her a good morning. She waved away her own best friend, dragging me by the wrist. My sister was mission oriented. Whatever was on her mind, I was going to be forced to listen once we found Peter. I didn't know what was up, but Mare was one of my best friends. So, whatever had her so tuned up was a big deal.

Peter was at his locker and looked up as we approached. Seeing my sister's expression as we got closer, he slammed the metal door shut with a clang and turned to give us his full attention.

"Hey, little brother!" my sister greeted him with the nickname she had given him and gave him a tight squeeze. "I'm glad to see you. I need you to tell Jace how much of a douchebag a guy can be."

He turned my way and deadpanned. "Boys are total douchebags, myself not included, of course." He turned to my sister and raised an eyebrow. "Is her lesson over now? I need to get to homeroom, I've had two tardies, and the third is detention."

"No. None of us are going to homeroom," Maris said, fuming. "We are now going to see that bastard, Ky Linley!"

I smiled. I couldn't help the little flip flop my heart did at the prospect of seeing him this morning. I sucked on my lips to try to hide my reaction, but when my sister wrenched my arm and growled, a grin replaced my smile.

"Don't be excited. This isn't going to be a social call. It's not going to be pleasurable for you either." Seeing my confusion, she shook her head and snorted an unhappy sound before starting down the hall with my friend and me behind her. A weird set of butterflies gathered in my belly. I wished I knew what was going on.

I saw him with a group of guys he always kept with, and they were all laughing, joking around like usual. Despite what my sister had said, I couldn't hide my smile at seeing him.

The other night flashed through my mind. He grinned, and I glanced at his mouth. Those lips had been on mine. I felt my face as it flushed, and I looked down.

Maris walked up to him and cut into his discussion. "We need to have a talk." He looked at me and smiled that smile that melted my insides.

He looked from me to Mare and shrugged. "Go ahead."

Peter slung an arm over my shoulder, Ky glanced at him and nodded a greeting, "Hey man, what's up?"

Before Peter got to answer, Maris shoved him in the chest. "We need to talk alone, Romeo." Ky's lips twitched into a sly smile, then he grinned and shrugged once more. He turned and slapped his best friend Alex on the shoulder before fist bumping another friend and sauntering away from the group to follow my sister. I looked back to notice

Alex watching my sister. She grabbed me once more in a death grip and dragged me behind her like I was a rag doll.

Leaning against the tile wall with such a lackadaisical attitude, that for a moment, made him look almost arrogant. I shook my head, shaking the thought away. Ky wasn't cocky. He was confident.

Just then he looked away from the ire on my sister to meet my eyes. His gaze slowly traveled down over my body, heating up as he looked at my breasts and non-existant hips. He licked his lips when he got to my sandals and seashell color painted toenails. I couldn't help the shiver that trembled up my spine.

Maris nearly wrenched my arm from my socket as she pulled me from his mesmerizing inspection. His eyes shifted her way and he cooly asked her, "What's up, Waverly?"

"*What's up?* Are you for real, Ky?" She smacked him with some real force in the chest, narrowed him with her killer, 'you're in shit now' look and said, "You're what's up, you neanderthal. You're telling the other JV football players that you slept with my sister over the weekend, and that she is sending you nude photos of herself."

I felt my cheeks burn.

What was my sister trying to do? This was the guy I liked, and she was embarrassing both of us. He would never say that.

I felt my belly butterflies take flight when he gave her that charming smile he reserved for teachers. I loved it. Mrs. French loved it too.

"Don't you think this is between me and Jacelyn, Mare. I don't think it's any of your business." He gave his lip a nibble, making me think of that kiss again.

"You're making my sister look like another one of your

tramps. That's my business. She's not a plaything or a point of gossip. I won't let you make her either. Kill the rumors, Ky." She gave him a look that lesser people would know promised death.

It was time to stop being a bystander, I resolved. I tugged at her arm trying to get her to look at me. "Mare. Ky wouldn't make up rumors about me sleeping with him. You heard wrong. Someone jealous started that stuff. It's not what it looks like."

My sister gave a sharp shake of her head. "No, Jace. It is what it looks like. He *is* the one saying those things, and *you* should know better."

Peter pulled me behind him now. Stepping in front of me, he tilted his head up to look at Ky's face. "That's low, Linley. I told Jacelyn that you were beneath her, but you proved to be even douchier than I had estimated."

With a lift of his shoulder and a roll of his eyes, Ky showed all the care in the world he gave for Maris and Peter's opinions regarding him. "Maybe you two should just let Jacelyn and me be. We were fine all weekend long without your interference."

Maris stuck her finger in his chest and got in his face. "Why? Why should we let you and Jace be? Is it because you can manipulate my sister like you've been doing because you know she has a crush on you? She's got stars in her eyes and wears her heart on her sleeve, whereas you just have no heart at all?"

He shook his head and smiled. "That's not what I'm saying."

Hearing this, I relaxed and returned his smile. Ky wasn't what they were making him out to be.

Then he continued. "Still, everyone knows... I only date girls that sleep with me. Jace wants me, and I want her. We have chemistry, it's only a matter of time now, a given, at this point. I didn't start any rumors. I just told people that I spent the weekend hanging out with Baby Waverly. People made their own conclusions."

I felt the blood drain from my face. I had no doubt that the only color left were my freckles, and I looked absolutely ghastly. My lips felt numb, and I had to swallow twice before I could choke out words. But finally I said, "You are better than this. You were flirting, but you didn't mean any of that bad stuff. You were being funny."

His eyebrow quirked, and then he glanced at the ceiling as if searching for divinity. "Jacelyn, you know who I am. What makes you think anything I said was a joke? I want you. I definitely want to see your body. Who wouldn't? You're hot as hell and growing up fast. You're beautiful and innocent and dying to be corrupted, and I want to be the one who does the corrupting. You like me, and I'm perfect for the job."

My sister shoved him so hard he stumbled back a few feet and crashed into the lockers, making a racket that echoed down the now empty corridor. "You're a filthy, fucking pig, Linley!" she screamed, causing a door down the hall to open as a teacher and a few students filtered out.

I looked around hoping the floor would suck me up, but there was no such luck. Fellsdale High School apparently had no sucking floors.

I sniffled, and Peter grabbed my hand. I glanced at my best friend to find him gazing at me with true sadness filling his eyes. "Come on," he said. "Let's get out of here."

"I wish I could be unborn," I murmured. It was worse than the humiliation. It was a heartache at losing the shine and wonder of who I knew Ky Linley was in my soul. He wasn't the guy who just behaved like that in the hall. I knew it. He couldn't be. My heart knew it.

"See, guys are douchebags and maybe we are both too young to date," Peter offered as consolation. "I say we swear them off until college."

two

. . .

Present day

I RAN a hand through my wet hair and shook it out, so it would air dry faster. I had my AirPods in, a towel on and the window open as I moved from the bathroom to my bedroom.

Peter, who was on the phone with me, huffed. "Not cool, Jace. You're officially cooler than me. You're a high school graduate now, while I still have another year to go. California changed you! You said it wouldn't, and now you are leaving me behind! You said you would *never* forget where you came from!" He emphasized the word like a soap star, and accompanied it with so much melodramatic sniffling that Mr. Ward, the drama teacher in Fellsdale, would be impressed.

"I left two years ago, it's not like I just up and left in the night," I argued.

"That wasn't the same thing. We were equal when you

moved away. We were moving at the same pace. Now you are ahead of me. You're going to be a college freshman with your sister in the fall. I'm going to be plain old Peter Kim come then." He sounded so disappointed by this outcome. I guess I shouldn't have surprised him with it.

"You are going to be Peter Kim in twenty years too." I shook my head, not understanding the argument.

"Whatever." His pout could be heard across the line. "Why aren't we vid-chatting?"

"I'm naked," I said, dropping the towel and grabbing my clothes. "Give me time."

"Ewww. Visual makes me wretch." He made a gagging noise and when I pulled my shirt on, I grabbed my phone and set it up on my phone stand before switching it to FaceTime.

"Awww, look there is your ugly face too!" I grinned.

My dad and I moved to San Diego at the end of my freshman year when his infidelity came to light, and he decided he was going to follow his heart here to be with a woman he met on a Classical Lit. Ed. forum. When he and my mom split, Maris stayed with my mom, and I felt awful that my dad would be alone, so I went with him.

I wasn't and still don't support all of his choices, but I love the man, and I saw this new chapter of his life imploding; I didn't want him out here afloat and abandoned when it did.

It took my dad six months to get an interim job at SDSU where Elena, the Lit professor worked, and it only took four weeks to see their chemistry tank. Now, he and I were out here and my family, who was once happy–dinner at night, camping trips in the summer, birthday parties and kisses–was torn apart.

"You could have done homeschooling too, hyeongje. It's

not like I did magic." I pulled my makeup mirror over and grabbed my brushes and got my makeup bag out.

"Don't Koreglish me, white girl. Your accent is atrocious, and you don't know how to use the words. As for homeschooling... My dad isn't a college professor who arranged for my introverted soul to do school without going to a classroom. I'm still jealous as hell." His head fell to the side, and he nodded like a little demented bobble head.

"You are not, you social butterfly." I applied eyeshadow primer. I would never be able to even out my freckles without a ton of concealer, which I hated wearing, but I can make my eyes look good with some color, liner and mascara.

"When you open your mouth like that, you look like a fish," Peter mocked me.

I stuck my tongue out at him, and then dropped the brush and grabbed the liquid eyeliner. With a practiced hand, I made a cat eye on my right eye, and then screwed up twice on my left eye as Peter watched.

"You didn't do school everyday for the last two years, I earned that diploma. Not to mention the fact that my dad wasn't teaching me. I did almost all of it myself." I exhaled and then stuffed the wand into its tube. "I worked hard."

"Okay, you might have more brains than me, but I still look better in a bikini." Peter grinned. A moment later, my message notification went off, and a photo came through of him and another guy in a speedo. They were pressed up to one another.

"Where was that?" I asked.

"It was a Party For A Cause at Filmore University a few weeks ago where LGBTIQA+ and allies got together. So many beautiful people." He sighed like it was a night to remember, which I bet it was. I also bet his mother would lock him back in the closet if she knew that photo existed.

Connie Kim was fed up with Peter. Last summer, she had taken him to Florida to meet the daughter of a friend. My friend, being who he was, convinced her to go to a party with him, and they both stayed out all night. As I understand it, the girl he was supposed to be courting came home hungover with hickeys all over, and her mother and Peter's parents' lost their minds. It was the end of the road since his mother has very little lassitude for his shenanigans.

"I don't think you are saying much, considering I've yet to grow into an adult body. I look like Tinkerbell. I'm just over five feet and finally a B cup. Thank God for mother nature," I murmured.

Peter hummed. "I've seen pics of you, Jacelyn. You grew up in all the right places. Even a gay boy can see you have curves."

"I'm curvy like you are," I argued.

"Whatever." He rolled his eyes. "So when will you be flying in?"

I sighed. I was going home. After two years away, I was returning to Fellsdale for the summer. I wanted to be there to see my sister graduate, then she and I could go off to State University together. It just so happened that, technically, I had graduated ahead of her.

My mom was excited that I was coming home. She was even more excited that my sister and I were going to continue our education. She had worked to put my dad through college and grad school, so she never had time to go herself. By the time my dad was stable and out of school and she could go, she'd had Maris and I, and she was up to her ears in Girl Scouts, soccer practice and school dances.

She never said it, but I know she regretted not having taken the opportunity to further herself beyond a housewife and a bartender. She slaved at a pub four and five days a week, ten hour days now. She was tired all the time, and the chance to go to school seemed way out of her grasp these days.

My secret fear? That I'll grow up to be just like her. Divorced, worked like a dog and heartbroken.

"I fly in on Thursday. I'm taking the red-eye. I'll be getting to Fellsdale at about eleven in the morning. Nothing flies directly to our neck of the woods from here. I have a layover in Newark." I purse my lips. "It's going to be weird coming back."

"Well, I don't have school on Friday. We had no snow days this year, so we have to use these up before graduation. We are getting off every Friday from now until the end of the year." Peter grinned. "We could meet up and gossip."

"Snow. Ewww! Don't miss it. And it sounds perfect to gossip on my first day back. Do you want to come over to my house?" I look through my lipsticks and glosses, searching for the perfect one. I make a face before he can answer. "I am stuck on the snow thing. I'm not going to be able to wear sandals all year anymore. What a bummer."

Peter snickers. "You're such a bitch, Jacelyn. I've not only got one more year to go, but I've been stuck in the snow the last few years, and you are complaining about your sandal sitch."

I laughed. "Well, when you put it that way, I haven't missed snow or high school in the last two years. Now, that is truly bitchy Jace coming to bat."

He sighed. "How did you ever even meet people in San Diego?"

"I think we've had this conversation before." I grunted, looking away and at the decor in my bedroom. The photos on the wall complimented the bedding and drapes. My dad paid a pretty penny to an interior designer to make the townhouse stylish until I was pleased. I might have been sticking it to him for what he had done to mom when I went for the really expensive stuff.

"Oh, right! You didn't meet people. You stayed inside while living in the land of sun, sand and tacos to do home-work all the time," Peter clucked.

"Not all the time." I made a face and pointed to my freckles that declared I went into the sun too much. "I also dated Javi, remember?"

I watched a smile blossom on his lips. "Javi, the surfer who let you take photos of him in and out of his wetsuit. The golden gloried god. But you broke up with him too."

"You make it sound like he was nude," I said, outraged.

"There was an awful lot of skin," Peter said, fondly.

I turned around and kicked the frame of my bed. "He was a surfer. He spent a lot of time in his trunks."

"But you didn't," Peter mournfully said, making a dirty joke that I ignored.

He and I talked about everything while we were apart. He knew I wasn't serious with Javier. I had made out with him, and we had some over the shirt groping action, but nothing more than that.

"And with that thought, I have to go, Peter. I need to drop off some books for my dad at SDSU. I'll be seeing you on Friday?" I asked.

"You better believe it, sister," he said.

I had taken up cooking since I left home. I loved it. It was both relaxing and distracting. Plus, I could be creative with it and experiment. My dad was home only a few nights a week, but I found I'd liked cooking for other people. I couldn't wait to return home to Maris and mom where it would be appreciated.

We hung up, and I looked around my room. Soon, I

would leave all this behind. I wasn't that sad about it. It felt like a waypoint rather than a place of my own. I had left home behind to come out here; I was feeling happy to finally be able to return. Even if it meant facing my sister, who hadn't forgiven me for leaving.

three

. . .

"ONE-ONE-THOUSAND... TWO-ONE-THOUSAND... THREE-ONE-THOUSAND..." I'd read somewhere that most planes have engine failure and crash within the first few minutes of take-off. I had taken to counting to thirty before I relaxed after the plane lifted-off. I took a deep breath and finished. "...Thirty-one-thousand."

I slumped back into my seat and smiled.

"These are pretty horrible seats, huh?" The man next to me grouched. I looked at him and grinned. He was in his late teens or early twenties, and he was nice looking. He had a stylish haircut and a sexy tattoo on his forearm that disappeared into his sweatshirt sleeve. I glanced down to see he wore skinny jeans and sandals. He was basically wearing a SoCal uniform. Yummy.

"Actually, I always pick the rear of the plane," I confessed.

His eyebrows furrowed, and his lips turned down. "Why?"

I couldn't help but bite my lip before admitting my

logic. "I've never heard of a plane backing into a mountain." I knew it sounded like a joke, but I was dead serious. I liked sitting where I had the most chance of surviving a potential crash.

Not to mention, I was close to the bathroom.

The man laughed at my reply and then raised his hand to high five me. "Alright, I can get behind that. I'm Austin."

"Jacelyn," I introduced myself. We hit it off, and I found he was a twenty year old college student who was returning home to the east coast. He was meeting friends in Newark, and they were all going to Florida on a road trip first before driving north again to their homes. He didn't seem put off by my age, and we exchanged socials and emails before the plane landed.

It was four thirty a.m. when we arrived in New Jersey, and I had a two hour layover before I would fly into the small airport back home in Pennsylvania. I said goodbye to Austin and promised to check his Insta for his travel pics. Making it to my gate with my Kindle loaded with books, I sat down to read one of my favorite authors. I had every intention of reading on the plane but was distracted with a guy that Peter would have drooled over.

For graduation, my dad had bought me a used 2019 Volkswagen Beetle in red to apparently match my strawberry blonde locks–which was not a cool joke. Red wasn't my favorite color and it didn't favor me, but the car was new to me, and I had to appreciate that. It was being shipped across the country by a car moving company. It was to arrive two weeks after I did. Maris still used my mom's, and it was a hassle for her because my mom worked a lot. My dad knew my sister wouldn't accept a car from him, so he asked me to share it with her, and I didn't mind that at all.

I was reading a great book about a girl who moved to

this town where there were elite people who were entitled to all these opportunities because they were related to the founders. I was enthralled and almost missed my plane boarding.

It was a quick hop to my next destination.

When I landed and deboarded, I walked through the security doors, looking down at my carry-on bag. "Jacelyn!" I heard my name called a second before arms wrapped around me and spun me around several times.

Maris. She always smelled like strawberry shampoo. My big sister was here, and it made me so emotional, that I hiccuped and teared up. She pulled away and laughed. "Dork." She wiped my face and kissed my cheek.

"Come on, let's go get your luggage. Do you have a lot of bags?" she asked.

My sister was as beautiful as I remembered. Her blonde hair shone. My hair looked like our grandmother's on our mom's side, and I wasn't a fan of the style on me. Whereas, it looked elegant on Grandma Virginia. All the women in my family had the same version of hazel eyes, but everything about my sister declared her as the stunner in the family. Mine were boring and dull, and looked a little more autumn-ish.

It was no secret that I envied her beauty, and I always wished I had a fraction of her beauty. I was just weird looking.

"I have three large bags. Dad is having the rest of my things shipped out with the car," I said.

My sister's lips flattened, but she kept her comments behind her teeth. I knew she didn't want to talk about him, not even to hear he was sending out my things. She was grudgy and done with him. I loved her, but my sister was stubborn. I couldn't help but think she would feel better about things if she would just learn to let go.

"Where's mom?" I looked around, wondering if she was somewhere else in the airport. She had said she was going to be here to get me.

Maris looked sad. "Sorry, Jace. Mom worked until two a.m. last night. I heard her up and down until sunrise cleaning for you to come home to an orderly house. I didn't wake her. But you'll see her when we get home. Don't be mad."

"I'm not!" I said. "Is she okay?"

"She's tired, and she works too hard. She doesn't make enough. Maybe she will get more money from that loser she divorced, now that you aren't living with him out there." Her words are bitterly spoken.

"Are you missing any after school activities?" I asked her. My sister is involved in a number of things. She did it to pad her college transcripts. If we had learned anything, it was she needn't have, since they accepted me without all the pomp and activity.

"I'm picking up my baby sister at the airport! There is nothing that I'm missing at Student Government right now that is half as important." She jumped up and down excitedly next to me, then grabbed my hand and held it until I joined her. We almost fell over laughing at our foolishness.

After we got my luggage, we struggled to pull it all out to the car. "We should have grabbed one of those carts," she groused.

My mom had an older model Ford Focus, the same car we had when we all lived together. I caught sight of a dent on the bumper and raised a brow. My sister grinned at me when she saw what I did. "I didn't see Grant Tenson's Jeep behind me at school one day. I did damage to mom's car, but

Grant's Jeep is built like a freaking tank. I didn't even scratch the paint."

I had never driven with my sister. Mom had warned me though. Maris was purportedly a bad driver. I had comprehensive collision coverage on the Beetle, so I wasn't that worried about my new car. I just wanted to be assured I would survive the drive.

"So, Jace, I don't want you to freak out, but I set you up with Alex's brother for tomorrow night. We're all going to Jimmy William's party. I've missed you so much, and I want to hang out with you. It will be so much fun. Peter can meet us there. You will love Trick. He's a little older than us, but he's great. It'll be awesome."

"Mare, you didn't." I sighed. I didn't want to start complaining within a half an hour of arriving home, but I couldn't help myself. "I don't want you to set me up with anyone. I just got back. I want to relax and settle into life here. I want to meet people on my own. Not to mention... What kind of name is Trick?"

"Jacelyn!" she said sharply. I looked down at my hands for a moment then got in the car. She piled my luggage in on her own and came around to the driver's side more calmly. "I swear, I'm not trying to set you up to go steady with Patrick. We call him Trick for short. It's just a night out. He's from Penn University. He just got home last week, and he's a good guy. He's not looking for a hook-up or girlfriend. Just someone to hang out with, so he's not a third wheel."

I sighed. "I wish you wouldn't. Please don't do it again. I would love to go out with you and Peter in the future, but don't set me up. I hate it. And I just got home. Do we have to go out with boys?"

She looked miserable. "School's going to be out soon and when it is, I don't know what is going to happen when

Alex goes to V Tech in August. I just really want the next few months with him to be bullshit free."

Seeing her face, I swallowed and nodded reluctantly. I know she loves Alex. He's her first love, her first everything. They've been together a year, and she fully expects him to break up with her and not do the long distance thing when they go to college.

She continued when I didn't offer more. "I swear, Jace, we will have a great time."

A pleading tone was in her voice, and I hated to hear it. We hadn't even reunited for thirty minutes, and I'd already made her sad. "It's fine. We'll go. You're right, it'll be fun. Plus, it will be good to go out and see familiar faces."

Maris smiled. She turned the key on the ignition of the Ford Focus and Ashnikko's "Worms" rocked through the interior.

four

. . .

"OH, this is going to be a fresh new hell. I'm going to hate it," I said, giving Peter a desperate look.

Peter refused to meet us at Jimmy's; instead he showed up to help me dress for a party, so I didn't wear 'sweats and a sleep shirt,' in his words.

Maris yelled up the stairs again. "Come down here, you two! Alex and Trick are here. We're all waiting on you!"

Alex was one of the rich kids, who was formerly a friend of Ky's. His dad was a realtor, and the man did really well around the resort areas here. We had tons of lakes that the 'summer' people liked to buy seasonal homes for, and they made the warmer months busy for local businesses.

As for his relationship with my sister, he'd noticed her at the beginning of their junior year, and he was boyfriend goals. She gushed about him non-stop. It helped that he never pulled the snob card that the rest of his crowd did. Maris claimed that no one ever said anything about him dating down a league, which pissed me off to hear that she even thought that he or anyone else might think that.

Peter pulled me close and grinned. "Alex is really cool,

Trick is an experience though. You can do this, slugger.
Make daddy proud."

"Ewww. Ewww, ewww, ewww. I'm not calling you
daddy." I cringed.

My best friend was attractive. His hair was grown out
on top and cut into a long pompadour type style that I
loved. His body was built better than most of the surfers I
hung out with back at Ocean Beach in San Diego. I wish I
was a guy because he was the whole package: witty, hot and
loyal.

"You'd like it, I promise." He wiggled his eyebrows
suggestively. I pretended to gag, and he laughed. "You are so
innocent. You need a good guide to the dirty side."

I sighed and opened my door. "A gay guide?" I asked.

He laughed. "Now that you mention it. I realize it's
your mustache that made me think you were a dude. You
need to get your upper lip waxed."

I flipped him off as I walked down the steps, hightailing
it down so my sister didn't explode waiting for us. At the
bottom of the stairs was a taller version of Alex, with light
brown hair and the same handsome smile. It was like a
dental ad, honestly. I expected to see a cartoon gleam and
sparkle to blind me when he gave me a second flash of his
chompers.

"Hello, Jacelyn. I'm Trick. Maris speaks about you
often. I feel like I know you already." He came forward and
folded me in a too forward hug.

I looked helplessly at Peter, who was trying not to
laugh.

I stepped back from his embrace and opened my mouth
to tell him the same thing out of politeness and realized I
couldn't. What would he say on the other hand if I told him
that Maris had never mentioned him to me, even once, until

yesterday? I ended up giving him a weak smile and nodding.

Peter, reading my discomfort, came to my rescue, and I could have kissed him for the kindness. "Well now that everyone knows everyone, why don't we go? It's going to be packed, and I want to stake out my part of the couch before anyone else does."

My bestie went to these things to people-watch and pick up on the gossip. He'd only met one guy he was interested in at a party since our small-time town didn't breed that many out of the closet types he could hook up with.

Maris nodded. "Yeah, we should go. Should we take two cars?" I looked at her. My eyes were pleading with her that we would all take one car, so I wouldn't be alone with the stranger she had set me up with. Peter spoke up then. "Jace and Trick can go with me and you and Alex can meet us there."

I relaxed. At least my bestie wasn't going to desert me with this guy.

When we were all seated in Peter's Elantra, Trick sat in the back with me like we were in an Uber and attempted casual conversation. "Mare says you finished high school early, that is exciting. You must be a smarty pants."

I made a face at the condescending tone. I shrugged rather than replying to the comment. Peter chuckled though. "Our girl is homeschooled. She graduated at the end of last month."

Trick's eyes ran over me in a creepy way. "How old are you?"

I pursed my lips a moment then replied, "I turned seventeen last August"

He grinned and nodded. "That's good, really good."

I raised my eyebrows. "It's good to be seventeen?" I

didn't know if I agreed with that, if it meant he thought I was old enough to be on the dating block.

Peter pulled out of our development and hit the gas. "How old are you?" He looked in the rearview mirror at Trick.

"I'll be twenty in September. I'm a Libra." He licked his lips and tilted his head in a way that made it look like he was bashful.

I turned my head and looked out the window. What kind of jackass told a girl their sign? I rolled my eyes and then heard my best friend snort. I looked at the rearview mirror and found him glancing back with glee in his eyes.

"Do you like long walks on the beach at sunset, Trick?" he asked the older boy, a little sarcastically.

I bit the inside of my cheek so I didn't laugh, but I heard Trick chuckle.

Silence filled the car, and I felt guilty for not making an effort. I took a deep breath before giving him another chance, "What's your major?"

"I'm a business major. I plan to eventually get my realtor license, but my dad thought it would be a good idea to get some business courses under my belt. We've talked about expanding what we can do." He nodded like he was agreeing with himself.

I didn't know what to add to that, so I just returned his nod. What did you say to someone that you had so little interest in?

Luckily, Jimmy Williams lived in a development not too many miles from mine. When we arrived there, I jumped out of the car and wrenched open Peter's door. I had to stop myself from grabbing his hand and running inside.

Trick slid out of the back and joined me, grabbing my hand like it was a real date. I forced myself not to pull out of his hold when he gave me that toothpaste commercial smile again. I tried to return it with something other than a grimace, but I didn't want any of this.

I was officially in hell, and it felt a whole lot like returning to home. Two years ago, I left this place where people told me who I was and made up stories about me. Now here I was, with Trick and Maris creating my future plans.

I glanced at Peter, who was laughing silently. He reached up and put his hand on the nape of my neck. He massaged it gently and pushed me in front of all of us. I swallowed and reminded myself I was doing this for Maris. I needed to be a good enough actress to make her happy.

We entered the house without knocking to find the music loud and the place packed. Trick asked if I wanted a cup and when I shook my head, he left to get Peter and I sodas.

"Peter! Can you believe him?" I gestured in Trick's direction and looked up at my bestie in distress. His face split into a grin, and his shoulders shook.

"He's not that bad. You're making a mountain out of molehill." He pulled me to him. "My little introvert can't socialize. It's okay. You're just out of practice. My goodness you are a mess at small talk."

We laughed together, and I cringed. He started pulling me to the couch when he saw an opening. There was only one cushion, but when we got there, Peter tilted his head in plea. The guy there laughed and held up a hand in greeting.

"Who is your friend?" he asked standing.

"Jacelyn Waverly." Peter waved in my direction as he fell into the cushions and pulled me down with him.

The guy looked at me and eyeballed me in surprise. "You're Maris' sister? Wow, you don't look like her."

I made a face and raised my eyebrows. "Nice way to suggest Mare has a troll for a sister," I joked.

"What?" He nearly swallowed his tongue and looked at Peter for help.

My friend's eyes sparkled. "It did sound like you were saying that."

"No! No. I meant... I mean... I was just saying... I am going to go." He hitched his thumb over his shoulder and backed away.

We held our serious expressions until he was out of sight, and then we broke down in guffaws of laughter.

Someone turns up the music for Saucy Santana and Latto's "Booty." It was so loud, we couldn't talk, so I looked around at the people and the scene. Nothing had changed in the time I'd been gone, except everyone was a little older. That realization was both settling and bothersome. I wanted things to be better here.

The song was turned down a few notches, and Peter leaned over and asked, "You doing okay?"

I gave him a small smile, at least I was with him. Things couldn't be bad with him next to me. For the first time in years, I didn't feel deserted and alone.

I glanced around and fell back into an old game we used to play. "So what do you think those two girls over there are saying?" I rudely pointed, so he knew who I was talking about, and he followed my hand. We've played this game since we were in junior high. We would watch people and make up our own dialogue or backstory based on their expressions and gestures.

The girls were typical of the Fellsdale area, poorly high-lighted dye-job, too much eyeliner and awful red lipstick.

"Which girl are you?" he asked.

"I'm the one on the left." I watched the darker haired

girl in the shorter skirt. We watched for a moment, and then I took up a silly tone and said, "I can't believe he came here with Rosa Easton, she is such a bitch!"

Peter laughed and played along, taking up the part of the girl on the right. "But did you see what she was wearing?"

"No! What is she wearing?" I continue watching the two girls.

"That blue mini that I've been dying to get from Forever 2 1." I smiled. Peter hated clothing from Forever 2 1. He thought it was the Wally World of the Mall. I don't know what was wrong with either Forever 2 1 or Walmart, but Peter hated both.

"OMG! She looks like a moo cow," I replied.

"I know. She has two Snausages for legs in that skirt, and it makes her ass look like the wide side of a barn," Peter scoffed.

I looked around until I found Rosa Easton and was surprised to find she had really grown into a beautiful woman. Her body was what boys would refer to as stacked and girls would be jealous over. She was wearing a short blue skirt. She didn't look fat, she looked like she was rocking some fine ass curves, and I envied her. She was beautiful.

Peter poked me and pointed to the two girls. "You know, I hear she eats nothing but Italian food, that's how she got so porky."

I laughed. My friend kept telling me to eat pasta to improve my curves. He said if I put on a little weight, my pants wouldn't fall off my butt. I don't really have that problem, but it's a running joke.

"I know he doesn't really like her," Peter said in his own voice. I followed his gaze to the guy standing with Rosa. He was a nice looking guy. Artsy looking. He had dark curly hair, very nice lips. I watched Rosa and the guy for a few seconds when he looked up and eyed Peter. I looked over to my friend and found Peter watching him with longing in his eyes.

"If he doesn't like her, who does he like?" I asked gently.

Peter's lip tilted up on one side. "I can't say. Gaven spends a lot of time in his closet."

I watched my friend for a moment, and then laughed quietly. I dropped our game for the scoop. "Is that so? Tell me everything! Were you in his closet with him?" I teased.

Peter motioned at zipping his lips and then smirked, before shifting his eyes from me back to Gaven. When he shrugged and looked back at me, I lifted a brow and sucked my lips. "You are such a bad influence."

I was just about to dig deeper into this topic, when Trick arrived back. He had two Dr. Peppers and a cup of beer. There was no room left on the couch, so he sat in front of us on the edge of the coffee table.

"Are you having a good time, Jacelyn?" He smiled the commercial worthy smile again.

"Yeah, you?" I popped the top on the can of soda he handed me.

"This isn't my style. I'm used to frat parties." He looked around, unimpressed.

"Are you in a frat?" Peter asked.

"I'm in SAE." Trick said, puffing out his chest. The reference is lost on me.

Not on Peter though. "Sigma Alpha Epsilon, that's a party frat. I guess this is rather junior high to you."

Trick chuckled. "It's tame for sure."

"Do you like being part of Greek society?" My friend continued small talk.

When he started replying, I tried to stay tuned-in, but there was something about Trick's voice that was boring to me. I soon zoned him out and started looking around after a few minutes into his dissertation about Greek life. I couldn't begin to express my thanks when Rosa Easton stepped up next to us, her eyes on him.

"Do you want to dance?" she asked him, biting her lip in a way she probably practiced in front of her bedroom mirror for hours.

Trick had the good grace to look torn. He started to shake his head, but I stopped him. "No, really, go and dance. Have fun with Rosa. Peter and I are going to sit here and catch up. You should have some fun."

He looked at me confused and like he wanted to argue, but before he did, I turned my head to Rosa. "Hey, girl. It's been a while. Trick is here from the Pennsylvania University, he deserves a good night. Hang out, please!" I probably sounded desperate.

Rosa didn't give him time to think more about it. She pulled him with her to where people were dancing and pushed her body to his. She looked over to me and winked. I gave her a thumbs up, and she grinned.

"Nicely done, Waverly." Peter held up his hand for a high five. "You just dumped your date off on a barracuda."

I hummed and leaned back into the couch, bumping shoulders with him. "This is nice. You and me, loud music and the smell of spilled beer."

He chuckled. "Definitely like... well not like old times. We were too young to go to these parties. But the next party we go to will be just like this one."

I looked up to find two drunk bodies grinding in the corner. "All the parties up until now have been you sitting on the couch missing me, right?" I teased.

"Yeah, you've been my heterosexual fantasy." Peter sighed, poignantly. "Actually, having you here makes me feel less out of place."

I wrapped my arm around his shoulder and pulled him to me to kiss his cheek. "I don't know what we would do without one another."

He snorted. "Well, I know I'm not as stimulating as homework every night, but you'll get by somehow."

I punched him in the arm, then looked around for more victims of our game. My eyes skimmed across the room and stopped dead as they met those of a figure standing against the wall by the kitchen door. I quickly glanced away and pretended I didn't see him. Ky didn't deserve my attention.

I could still feel him looking at me though. I hated that it still gave me a flush of pleasure to have his attention. It was too much temptation though, and I looked back at him and stared.

He had changed. He was bigger, more built and solid. He still had those light gray eyes and black hair, but his face was more masculine now, more grown up. He wore a black t-shirt that molded to a muscular chest and arms. His jeans hung low on his hips, and he stood there like he was going to pounce on me, one shoulder dipped lower than the other and one foot ready to push off the wall.

Ky Linley was beautiful, but he had always been. I wanted to kick him in the crotch and see if it ruined his aura.

"Hmmm... that is not a promising start, Jace." I heard Peter say next to me.

I couldn't reply. I was under the spell, all over again, of the guy who ruined my reputation. What was it about him that I wanted to let him do it again?

My bestie continued his commentary. "Don't let Maris

see you looking at Ky like that, or she will castrate him and have you married off to Trick before the week is out."

I turned to look at Peter, trying to focus on him. I felt light headed. "Is it warm in here?" I asked, embarrassed that my voice sounded weak.

Peter shook his head then looked back at Ky. "Why couldn't you like Mr. 'I'm a Libra', Waverly? You just can't stop loving trouble no matter what he does."

"I know he's a jackass, but... I don't know what's wrong with me." I looked back at Ky, but he wasn't looking at me anymore.

"There are no 'buts', girl. He's just a jackass, and he went through dozens of girls after you. He screwed most of the female junior and senior class during his sophomore year. You are going to have to go to asshole rehab at some point. You really have to kick the habit." Peter looked disappointed.

I knew everything he said was true.

But there was one thing I was very aware of at the moment, looking at Ky Linley made me feel like I was still crazy for him. I still held hope that he wasn't the guy he acted like.

And I knew that made me dumb, but I still wanted him.

five

. . .

"SO MAMA WAVERLY, what do you think of this one?" Peter pushed my laptop in front of my mom. She was a laid back woman. There was no 'Mrs. Waverly' with her. She had been insisting all my friends call her 'mom' since I was a little kid. Peter, who had continued to visit while I was gone, had been quizzing her for some time on guys he thought were hot. Even though she acted like she was only putting up with the practice, she was really having a lot of fun with it.

"He's pretty, Peter. Not very masculine though, is he?" my mom said, tilting her head.

Peter squinted and studied the photo for a long moment.

My mom continued though, "The guy next to him shows promise. Don't know about the pink hair though."

He skims his hand over his pompadour. "You don't think I should dye my hair pink then?"

With a roll of her eyes, my mom chuckled. "No. Connie would not appreciate that." Connie, Peter's mom, had worked with my dad at Holymount College before we left.

She was a mathematics professor, and was civil, but not accepting of the rift in my family. She whole-heartedly believed that a family did not divorce.

I also think she believed that I turned Peter gay. She needed to blame someone, and I was as good as anyone. Truth was, that Peter knew more about his sexuality than I did at the time he came out. I was still confused about what boys and girls did together when he became aware of the fact that girls did nothing for him. It definitely wasn't my ultra liberal thirteen year old self that made him aware of who he was. If anything, it was the other way around.

"What do you think, Jacelyn? Maybe a pink fringe?" Peter smirked.

"I think you could pull off a soft ash blonde. I think blond Asians are hella hot. I wouldn't say no to a hot Asian asking me out." I shrugged and messed up his hair.

"If we started dating, my mother would think you were a divine blessing and that dying my hair was the least of her worries." He laughed.

"I still wouldn't be Korean," I said. Connie was holding out for a Korean match for him.

"But you are a girl, Jace," he said, flicking the end of my hair with his finger. "Some concessions could be made to save my mother from seeing me one day in a lip lock with a broad shouldered, football playing male who had tight glutes."

My mom fanned her face. "When you describe it like that. I want to sign up for one. Are you two going out today?"

I nodded and got a soy yogurt from the fridge. "Don't know where yet. I need a job."

"I have to work all weekend, and all next week I work super swing from four in the afternoon to two in the morning. I won't be seeing all that much of you kiddos around." She reached out and drew me into her arms, almost crushing my yogurt between us.

I worried about my mom working so much. She looked tired, and I felt like part of that was my dad's fault. She hadn't sued for child support or custody, and he had only offered her a small amount in the divorce settlement. He sent some for Maris every other month, but not much. Mom was literally killing herself to support her and my sister here in Pennsylvania. Meanwhile, my dad gave me a beautifully decorated room and a newer car in San Diego.

"Well, if it will help out, I can start cooking meals for everyone. And once I find a job, I can pitch in for groceries and utilities," I offered.

My mother smiled at me. "I'll take you up on making breakfast, but you just got home, you don't have to rush out and find work. And you don't have to pay for anything, I make enough to get us by. I don't want you to spoil your summer. You're a good egg, Jacelyn Waverly. Thanks for offering." She leaned over and hugged me hard, before grabbing her purse and heading out.

"I suppose you want me to drive you around, so you can look for employment because the Miss Goody-Two-Shoes in you can't let your mom be the sole provider." Peter grabbed an apple from the bowl on the counter and tossed it in the air.

I nodded and said. "I'm going up to change. I'll be down in a few minutes."

Maris was still sleeping off last night's party. She got home early this morning, with Alex carrying her in his arms. My mom didn't seem worried about Mare staying out late. When I raised the topic this morning, my mom smiled tiredly. She gave me a weary look and said she wasn't going to sit on us and make us stay home. She had to go to work and couldn't be home to watch our every move. She trusted us to take care of ourselves and not cause trouble and to make good decisions. She wasn't going to lay down the law with a curfew she couldn't enforce. She just hoped we would respect her enough to not walk all over her faith in us.

As I was fixing my make-up, I looked at a photo on my corkboard. It was taken my last year here, and I'd never taken it down. It was of Peter, Maris and I in the lunchroom and in the left hand corner, Ky was looking at me. It made me think of the night before.

He was still beautiful and as of last night, still looking at me. Just thinking of him made me have butterflies. I was both hoping and terrified I would see him again.

Peter was right. Ky was an asshole, and I had to keep in the forefront of my mind that he made my freshman year hell. I could hope that there was a twelve step program for addiction to bad boys. Maybe their prayer would be, "God grant me the serenity to accept the things I cannot change, change the things I can and the ability to know an asshole from a good thing when I see it."

Right now, I was convinced I didn't know the difference.

Giving myself a once over in the full-length mirror that hung on the back of the bathroom door, I gave myself the rating of six out of ten and headed downstairs. Peter had moved on to watching Kpop videos on my laptop, holding up a finger asking me to wait as he sang along to "Oh My God" by G(I -DLE).

I checked my bag to make sure I had everything while he watched the video, and I watched him as he did the dance the women in the video were doing.

"I don't know, Jace. These songs sound so good in Korean, but when you translate them to English, it's so cliche and corny." Peter moved his hands over his head in this ridiculous twirl that made me smile. I missed my bestie for reasons like this.

"So just listen to it, and pretend you don't know English," I reasoned.

"Just might work," he said, grabbing his keys, at the same time as he closed the lid of my laptop. I wrote Mare a note, and we headed out.

The Camry was a hand me down from his dad. When they got a new car last year, they gave him this one on the understanding he would attend church with them on Sundays and keep it clean. One of those things happened. The inside of the car was neat and tidy.

I slipped into the passenger side and fastened my seatbelt.

"Where to first?" Peter asked, turning the car around in a three point turn.

"Any place that might be hiring. I have no pride nor shame since my mom is overworked, and my dad has single handedly brought her to the brink of hell on Earth." I tapped my fingers to the beat of the music playing quietly from his CarPlay. It was Labrinth's "Never Felt So Alone", one of my favorites.

"Stop it, Waverly!" Peter gave me a look of joking censure. "Things have yet to get so bad that you have to work at Walmart!"

I ignored his teasing. My mom really was slowly killing herself with all the hours she was taking on. I bit my lip, "Let's start at the mall in Maystown."

Peter nodded but didn't look excited about going downtown. "I'm sure you will hit something there. You look like a Hollister girl."

I made a face. I knew clothes were a big deal to people here. Name brands and hot logos meant something. You could get by in San Diego with shorts and tank tops from vendors on the beach or Target. I really stopped worrying about what I was wearing. The West Coast is really more laid back and slower paced. There are still label snobs, but you can get away with being comfortable over fashionable.

Of course, if I had to be a label ho here to earn money for my family, I wasn't going to make a fuss. If it fed my mom and sister, I'd make it work.

Peter and I spent a few hours at the mall. I ended up talking to a dozen shop managers, and I filled out even more applications. I was disappointed to hear that most places wouldn't be hiring for another month. I knew thirty days didn't sound like a lot, but that was a lot of money that wasn't coming into the household in the meantime. I still had to put gas in my car when it got here.

"Are you hungry?" Peter asked, smiling.

I nodded because I was starving. "I could eat a horse, and I'm still not eating red meat."

"Weirdo," Peter replied, pulling my arm. "I know where to take you."

"Wait, the food court is in the other direction." I tugged my wrist in his grasp trying to get him to change his course.

"We're not eating here, Jace. Come on." Peter's smile promised that he had a surprise for me. I knew from many years of friendship that he wouldn't give up so much as a hint, so I let him lead me back to the car.

We left Maystown and headed back to Fellsdale, and we were on a familiar route when I began to figure out where we were going. Piero's was an Italian restaurant that was in town. I loved their pizza and while I was gone, I'd often lamented the fact that I missed the slices from the restaurant.

When we pulled into the parking lot, I let out a laugh. "You just leveled up to an awesomely cool best friend.

"Still not a high school graduate, kinda cool, but I agree, I'm cooler than most." He smirked.

We made it inside and got seated at a booth when a girl I remembered vaguely, Madison Rhiner, came to take our order. She casually greeted Peter like they knew one another, and treated me with a friendliness most service people reserved for clients.

"I'll have pineapple, onion, and spinach. Can I get goat cheese on that?" I asked, smiling happily.

Across from me, Peter stuck his fingers in his mouth and pretended to gag. "Won't eat meat but will get boob cream on her pizza."

"Yeah. What size?" Madison asked, smiling at our ribbing one another.

"Extra large," I replied. What I didn't eat, I would take home and Maris and my mom could pick at or I'd have it to eat for later.

Peter smacked his menu on the table. "I'll have a Ceasar's salad and a chicken parm sandwich."

"Murderer," I grinned, teasing him.

"You know it. I also eat their unborn babies," he said, grinning.

I missed this so much. I loved this friendly banter.

When Madison left with our order, my eyes followed her. I noticed that the inside was the same as when I had left, but there was a new dining room extension that was a sunroom that was closed for seating at the moment. The area we were sitting in had red wallpaper and wood accents.

The tables had white clothes underneath with a red angled one on top. And the aroma of the restaurant was heavenly: garlic, onions and tomato sauce filtered out from the kitchens.

"Did you see the sign in the window?" Peter pointed to the same window that had the neon 'OPEN' sign and below that was one that said 'Now Hiring: Inquire Within'. "It would be awesome if you worked here. We could pig out all the time. I get sick of healthy food at home."

I waited until Madison came back to ask her about the sign. She said they had two positions open: prep worker in the kitchen and waitress in the front. I knew nothing about waitressing, but I could definitely do kitchen work. I asked her if there was anyone I could talk to about the position, and she went to get the owner.

With three pieces of pizza stuffed into my belly, I was feeling full. I leaned back just as an older man approached the table. "Jacelyn? I'm Ricky Piero. Maddy tells me you're looking for a job. When you are done eating, let the hostess know, and we can have a talk in my office."

I smiled. "I'm done. We can talk now."

His lips tilt up on one side. "I need to check the deliveries. Give me five. I'll be out in a few."

When he walked away, Peter kicked me sharply under the table.

"What?" I asked, rubbing my shin with the other foot.

"I was joking! I hope you realize that working here means seeing everyone you went to school with. All the haters, all the baiters."

"I haven't lived here in two years. I really couldn't care less about the haters anymore. I forgot all the reasons they had for not liking me and baiting me. I need a job, this is close to home and perfect." I paused for effect. "Not to mention. Free pizza!"

Peter wiped his mouth and nodded at the pick-up counter. I looked over, and Shea Reilly was there. I always found her to be ridiculous, even if she was incredibly beautiful. She was the kind of girl who knew it and was insufferable for it. All the guys in our school wanted her and if rumors were true, quite a few had her. She was one of those entitled people that was crass and lewd.

Despite all that, I could live with her as a customer. I shrugged at Peter in response.

Madison brought Peter another soda and escorted me to Ricky's office—a small area covered in papers on the desk and invoices pinned to the wall. There was an out of place puppy calendar on the wall that he clearly used to pen in deliveries and stick post-its to for time off. He was a hot mess.

"Will you be able to work after school?" he asked, sitting back in an old school office chair that sounded like it would break at any moment. He gave me his undivided attention.

I smiled. "I graduated early, in April. I need a job to help my mom out, and I can work any hours, although I have to make arrangements for rides until my car arrives from the moving company."

He doodled on a piece of paper and nodded. "Do you have experience waitressing?"

"I don't, I'm better fit for the kitchen, and I am a quick learner." I tried not to let a thread of desperation leak into my voice.

"I think this will work. Can you start tomorrow night? I'll need you to stay until midnight. It's an hour after we close for clean up. I'll give you your schedule then." He held out his hand to shake mine, and I grinned.

"Thanks, Mr. Piero." I nodded.

"You can call me Ricky."

I left feeling pretty proud of myself and more giddy when I learned our food had been comped.

"So, I guess it went well?" he asked me as we got in his car.

I nodded and laughed happily. "I got the kitchen prep position."

"So, I assume I'm driving you to work tomorrow?" Peter asked.

"You are!" I smiled gratefully.

six

. . .

I REALIZED Sunday night that I had never asked what to wear, and had no idea what was acceptable. I went safe with a pair of jeans and a plain green t-shirt, without a logo on it. I pulled my most supportive trainers on with cute pizza socks on them, smiling at the special touch. Brushing my hair, I pulled it back into a braided bun, the small curls that sprang free rogue around my face weren't something I could control, and I tried to pin them back with bobby pins. I spent twenty minutes on my makeup, so I could look more confident than I was feeling.

On my way out, I left a note for Maris who was out with Alex, hurrying when I heard the horn honk from Peter's Camry.

The second I slid in and clipped myself in, Peter turned down "Slow" by Jackson Wang & Ciara. Turning to me, he raised an eyebrow. "Are you excited to become an employed teenager?"

I laughed and nodded. "It's going to be the first night in a life of hard labor from here on out," I joked.

"You'll be able to buy me many pretty things, though." Peter fluttered his eyelashes and put the car in reverse.

I nodded. "That's why I got a job, so that I can gift you with expensive and frivolous items that you will toss aside without thought when a new shiny bobble catches your eye."

"We've got this plan down pretty well, Waverly," he said.

The song ended, and I turned down the next one, which is an older Kpop song by a boy group I can't stand. "What are you doing tonight?"

My friend's mischievous look made me laugh. It told me one thing. "It's a boy! Are you going out with someone?"

He gave me a coy look before returning his focus back on the road. We don't have much time to chit chat since Piero's isn't far from my house. He sighed happily, "I'm staying in with someone."

"Is it someone I know?" I probed.

Peter shook his head. "Nope. I can tell you nothing. You know I'm gay, but no one knows he is, and because I really like him, I'm not sharing his secret with a soul. Not even someone I trust with the secrets of my soul."

"You trust me with your soul secrets?" I asked. "Awww. I think you should let me cut your hair."

"Secrets of my soul, Jace. Not my vanity." He blew a raspberry and pushed me away.

"I trust you will remember to be safe." I gave him a serious look.

Peter rolled his eyes. "Yes, mom. I'll also remember to say please when I want a kiss and thank you before I leave, too. Don't worry, I know the etiquette for visiting someone's house."

I chuckled. "Sure you do."

When we arrived at Piero's, I hugged my friend and thanked him for the ride. "Are you sure Maris and Alex can pick you up at midnight? I would, but it's a school night. Connie lays down the law at eleven p.m., and I think if I'm out too late Dalnim will come for me. Have fun!"

"Yep, you too, you ho-bag!" I said getting out. I had butterflies as I reached the restaurant door and put my hand on my stomach and took a deep breath before pulling it open.

Madison met me with a smile. "Come on in!"

She led me into the kitchen, and I found a clean and orderly workspace. Madison's eyes widened. "This is Melissa, she's the lead cook and kitchen manager."

Melissa didn't say much. She wasn't unfriendly, just brusque, and didn't seem to believe in small talk. "I have a line cook, but he does deliveries too. You're food prep. Unfortunately, for your first night, our dishwasher is out sick. I am going to need you to do food prep and dishwashing. Do you have a problem with that?"

I shook my head. "It would seem that the more things I learn, the more help I'll be."

She looked me over and gave me a nod of approval.

Ricky came in a few minutes later and asked me to go with Madison and go over the menu, so Melissa could continue to work on tickets until the line cook got back from a delivery. I followed her out, and she stopped at a closet and got me a t-shirt that she told me to pull over my own that said Piero's Pizza with the logo over the right breast. On the back, it had a cartoon pizza chef with a pizza pie coming out of the oven. The color was red and with the green t-shirt I already wore underneath, I looked Christmas-festive.

Madison grinned. "Okay, you can read the menu on your own. You don't need help with that. You do need to know that Wednesday, Friday and Saturday, there is a hostess here. Her name is Angelina, and she wears too much perfume and is a walking pair of fake boobs.

"You need to stay away from Artie, the busboy, he's handsy. He's Ricky's nephew and thinks he's untouchable, but he's got a pair of nuts and if he corners you, knee him in them and don't be afraid to make a fuss. He's going to be disgusting and call you 'hot babe' and talk about your body whenever Ricky's not around. His day is coming.

"Lastly, is your kitchen co-worker. Time for me to objectify... total babe. I'll leave you to discover him on your own. If only I were five years younger." She sighed dreamily and grinned.

I held up the menu, "What am I supposed to have gone over on this with you?"

"What we offer." She nodded.

I raised my eyebrows and chuckled. "Has the menu changed much in two years?"

"Only a dish or two, why?" Madison asked.

"I grew up eating here. I think I learned to read by studying this menu," I joked.

She pulled it out of my hand and bonked me on the head with it. "Well then, it will look like I did my job."

I returned to the kitchen, and in quiet company, made salads, sliced meat, took things out of a very orderly put together freezer, and put things into an equally arranged refrigerator. It was a simple and straightforward job of following easy directions. This was literally a cherry work position, and I was thankful to have landed it.

Melissa nodded toward a silver bin of marinara sauce. "Jacelyn, would you refill the marinara?"

Just then, the kitchen door swung open and Ricky

walked in with a familiar figure behind him. I froze in my place, and I could feel my eyes widen comically.

"Jacelyn, this is Ky, our delivery driver. When he's not making deliveries, he'll be back here with you and Mel as a line cook. He knows this kitchen almost as well as she does. He also waits on tables, buses, and can host. If I ever drop dead, he can probably handle my end too. If you have any questions, this is who you go to."

Ky's lips tipped up on one side, not really a smile, just a suggestion that there could be one. He nodded my way. "We know one another."

I expected him to say more. He didn't do anything but reach for an apron and ask Ricky, "Where do you want me?"

"Would you give Melissa a break? She's been here since two, and she's not been off her feet." Ricky smiled and headed down the hall to his office, as if it was a given that Ky was taking over.

Melissa removed her apron and hung it on the hook. "Nothing is in the oven right now. You somehow came in at the perfect time for a switch. There are two tickets for pick up dates of seven and seven-thirty. Jacelyn has most of the prep work done for the rest of the night. Maybe teach her how we make fresh marinara."

Neither of them are aware that I'd begun sweating, and my heart rate was through the roof. It's ridiculous to die on your first night of work from panting to death. But what are the chances of me getting a job where I work with Ky? I'll tell you. In my case, it's fifty-fifty.

"I saw you the other night," Ky said the second we were alone.

I wanted badly to be casual and appear sophisticated. The truth was, this was one of those occasions people prayed their deodorant was working, and that their makeup didn't appear garish in the fluorescent lighting. I was also hoping that my breath didn't smell.

I swallowed the lump in my throat and proceeded to drop two onions, as I attempted to carry them to the prep area. I cleared my throat. "I saw you too. It's been a long time," my voice sounded forced.

I kept telling myself to act natural, but I took in his backwards ballcap and the way his jeans fit him, and I felt warm... too warm. Peter wasn't the only one who liked broad shoulders and nice glutes.

I came down to one conclusion, God was punishing me for all the naughty things I did as a child.

Or maybe Karma was an activist, and she was coming around to slap me in the butt for the fact that I hadn't dated more in San Diego. Obviously, I squandered my opportunities to get over him, and now I was being tortured in whatever circle of Dante's Inferno of Hell this kitchen at Piero's was.

"You look good," he said with a smile. And if my heart beat any harder, the people in the dining room would hear a bass drum.

"You're graduating soon?" I asked, as I shredded a piece of lettuce with my hands. I had nothing better to do with them.

"Yeah. Four more weeks and I'll be done. Are you going to be coming back to FHS now?" He scraped the area Melissa rolled dough out with a sharpened looking tool and cleaned the area.

I shook my head, although he wasn't looking at me. "No. I graduated early. I did homeschooling and advanced my studies. I'm done."

I watched Ky as he paused and turned back to me. "You already graduated?"

I smiled at the disbelief in his voice. It always felt good to surprise the people around here. It wasn't that they had discounted me in any way, but it always felt good to exceed what their expectations were of me. "Yeah, I finished in April. I'll be starting college in the fall with Maris."

"Wow." He grinned. "And you already picked a college too? It's impressive all that you've accomplished. To think all I've done is plugged along at school, played some sports and delivered a few pizzas."

"You haven't chosen a college yet?" I was starting to settle down. The butterflies in my stomach were no longer the size of pterodactyls and my breathing was back to normal. Talking to him was becoming easier.

"Oh, no. I'll be with you and Maris at state school. I need to stay close to my family. I applied to a few different schools. I had a football scholarship to UWV 'Go Mountaineers!' but I can't go that far away. I also had another scholarship to go to Dartmouth, but that's too far too."

"How do you know what school I'm going to?" I asked, curiously.

"Your sister mentions it all the time at school. Plus, she's wanted to go to State since she was in elementary school and has been bragging that you were going together. I just didn't realize it was now." He gave me a look, clearly impressed.

I shook my head and under my breath, but loud enough to be heard said, "Stalker."

He talked a bit more about school, and then got quiet. I listened and tried to remember that he was a jackass, but in this environment and chatting with him here, it was easy to forget he was a slimy human being.

Clare Lukas

I desperately needed to remember that because I was susceptible to his brand of jackass.

"What was the Dartmouth scholarship for?" I ask.

He gave a wicked grin. "Academic. I know I look good and can catch a football like a fucking boss, but believe it or not, I can add and subtract, diagram sentences, I know what happens to an acid when it comes in contact with a base, and I excel at anatomy."

I looked down at the lettuce I'd been shredding to find it a pile of ungodly small parts. I moved away from him and grabbed a tomato. Under my breath, I prayed, "God, grant me the serenity to accept the things I cannot change, change the things I can and the ability to know an asshole from a good thing when I see it."

Ky must have bat-like hearing because he laughed. "You doing a twelve step program?"

"Yes, I've joined Jackass-Addicts Anonymous," I murmured.

He laughed. "So you're saying I have a chance."

"I don't have an Academic scholarship," I threw it out there to change the topic.

"Do you need a tutor in anatomy?" he teased me.

"I'm sure you've been studying with dozens of girls, but I'm not interested in being associated with your rumors or locker room talk. I might not have a scholarship, but I'm not dumb enough to be burnt by you twice." I sliced the tomato with a definitive force and began to ignore him.

Madison stuck her head in. "Ky, there are two calls for deliveries. Finish up what is on those tickets, and these are up. One is going to the lake, so you have a long trip out and back. I'll grab Melissa and let her know she's going to have to come back in fifteen."

Ky nodded to her and finished the food he was

preparing, then started manipulating the dough for a pizza. We worked in silence until Melissa came back and took over. She and Ky went over where he was in process, and she nodded.

I grabbed a carrot and started grating them, imagining the vegetable was Ky's face when I heard a throat being cleared behind me. "I know I left you with a bad impression of me. I'm really not a bad guy, you don't have to feel so uncomfortable. I swear to you, I won't really bite or overstep. I will flirt, but it's meant to be fun. I was an asshole when I was a kid. You don't know it, but you taught me a lot about girls."

I smiled at that wryly. Ky was a nice guy?

That was somewhat hilarious, I hadn't realized before that he had such a command of comedy. "I remember just how nice you are. I doubt the change in you, and I hold no surprise in your scholarly astuteness of anatomy. Just because I think you look good, and you make me get butterflies, doesn't mean I will ever forget what's required to be a girl you will look at twice or be with once."

His smile slid from his face, and he looked sad, heartbroken even. He looked over my shoulder as if searching for the right words and being unable to find them, his shoulders fell, and he backed away.

"Ky, these deliveries are ready," Melissa reminded.

He grabbed them and headed out. She shot me a look that seemed oddly disappointed and went back to work.

seven

· · ·

I'D BEEN WORKING at Piero's for a week, and it was the following Friday when Peter dropped me off with the promise he would pick me up after my shift at midnight. He had another date with his mystery man, and I was very curious at this point, but he had asked me to stop asking. I had curbed my curiosity and held my tongue–it was killing me not to ask.

The kitchen was busy, but Melissa was in a good mood. She had the *I Heart Radio* station on, and we were listening to the *80's and 90's Hit Factory*. Ky was dancing around and singing into a carrot, as Melissa sang into a ladle. "Do you believe in life after love?"

I laughed and replied with the next line. "I can feel something inside me say..."

We all sang the next part together, "I really don't think I'm strong enough, no!"

Melissa chuckled and pointed to Ky. "I know he's got all these songs down after working with me. I'm surprised you know that one though."

"My grandma and mom love Cher," I confessed. "My

mom says my grandma drove her around in her Chevy Nova when she was a kid and played non-stop Cher and Quarterflash. I also know the lyrics to all their songs."

She cackled. "Good to know. That's a little earlier in the 80's than my time, but I might have you sing for me at some point."

Ky opened his mouth to add to the conversation, but Ricky stuck his head in the kitchen. "Waverly, personal call. I'm going to allow it because it affects your ride tonight, but try not to make a habit of it. We're running a business."

My eyes widened, and I felt my heart thunder. I hated getting in trouble, and this was the sort of thing that drove me to feel like I had messed up big time, even though I did nothing wrong.

My hands shook as I picked up the phone in the kitchen and hit the blinking button indicating the call was on hold. "Hello?"

"Jace?" It was Peter. I sighed.

"I can't be getting calls at work, you have to know that!" I scolded. "Can we talk when you get here?"

"Actually, that is why I'm calling. I'm really sorry, I'm out somewhere with my date, and I just got permission from my parents to spend the night with... well, not him, but that's where this is going. Do you want me to call your mom or Maris?" he offered.

I clunked my head against the wall. "My mom's working, and Mare is away tonight at some party at Filmore College with Alex. I'll call Trick or see if Melissa can take me home."

"I'm sorry, don't hate on me for this. It's so important to me." I could hear the pleading in his tone. It *was* important to him.

"Don't worry about it. It's okay. Enjoy your date," I said

and hung up, a whole less jovial than I had been a little while earlier.

When I got my break, I tried to call Trick but got no answer. I left a message but had no real expectation that I would hear back from him. At midnight, the doors were locked because Piero's stayed open an hour later on Fridays and Saturdays. I made sure it was okay with Ricky that I carried around my cell. I tried to call Trick twice more, and then finally asked Melissa if she could give me a ride.

"Babe, I would, but I'm heading out to Pour Lenny's for a drink with some friends, and it's in the other direction. It's already late, and I don't want to miss them before closing time. Ky will take you home."

I turned when I heard a sound of agreement. Ricky stood there. "As a matter of fact, I'll put you on the same hours this week, so he can bring you in and take you home. It will be easier on everyone. Your friend Peter won't have to go out of his way."

My eyes flew to Ky, and he looked hopeful and uncomfortable all at once.

"I don't want to impose," I tried to bow out.

Ky shook his head. "It's no imposition, and it makes sense. I'll be a complete gentleman."

Ricky nodded and pointed at him. "Damn right you will be. Not just your job will rely on it."

I didn't know what that meant, but I watched Ky take a deep breath and nod solemnly.

Ricky then walked around the kitchen checking on things. Finding everything satisfactory, he smiled and gestured for me to be the first one out of the kitchen and I went to the back, used the ladies room and grabbed my things from my locker.

When I came out, Ky was seated in a booth at the front

of the dining room. He was tracing patterns on the table glass with his finger, and I swatted his arm. "Madison Windexed all the tables before she left."

"Morning shift redoes them." Ky grinned and stood.

I had a bad feeling inside me. This just wasn't a good idea for my Jackass Addiction Program. I was already giving into weaknesses when we worked together. Now we'd be spending more time together.

I closed my eyes and made a promise to the universe that in the morning, I would actively start looking for good guys to date. I would try to get my fascination with this bad boy under control.

"You ready to go?" he asked with a raised eyebrow.

I didn't want to open my mouth and say something stupid, so I nodded and walked behind him to the exit. When we made it outside, I realized that despite him doing deliveries and me working there a week, I had no idea what he was driving.

I waited for him to tell me which way to go.

"You really hate this, don't you?" he asked quietly.

"NO!" I said forcefully. Then sighed in defeat. "I don't know. I don't trust you. I definitely don't trust the way you look at me. There are a million things I tell myself to be careful of when it comes to you so that I don't repeat the mistakes of that stupid girl I was when you played me the first time. So if you could just take me home, and not... Just take me home, please." I shook my head. "Where's your car?"

"Jace, I..." He sighed before leading me to a maroon muscle car. Unlocking my door, he opened it and stepped back. I tried not to be impressed with the chivalry.

"This? This is what you drive? You make deliveries in this?" I said, peering at the interior.

He chuckled. "No, I use Ricky's Honda Civic for deliveries. This is my car, I don't drive the delivery car home."

"What is this thing?" I knew little about cars, I could tell a sports car from a minivan, and a truck from a compact, of course–but whatever this was, it had to be something special, it was a sweet ride.

"It's a 1973 Dodge Charger SE Brougham. My dad and I have been restoring it over the last few years. It's kinda a labor of love, and a lesson in distraction." Ky appeared proud of the car, and if he and his dad had actually restored it and it wasn't some pick up line, he should be.

I decided to go for the low blow. "This must get you a lot of girls."

His face fell, and he shook his head. "I don't use my car to get tail. I know you don't believe me, but I'm not that stupid ass kid I was in my sophomore year. I had to grow up. I didn't get to go on being young, dumb and full of—"

"Ewww, don't finish that statement." It was vile, and I'd heard older boys say it, I didn't need to hear it said again.

He watched me for a second and nodded, saying nothing more before closing my door. He walked around slowly, and I watched as he took a deep breath and unlocked his door and slid in. The awkward silence was killing me as he put the key in the ignition and started the car. The engine growled, and the car rumbled beneath me.

I didn't have to tell him where I lived. As kids, he'd been to my house countless times. He and Maris had grown up as friends.

What would my sister say if she knew I was in a vehicle with Ky Linley right now? She would probably have an embolism.

The silence was killing me. "Are you still going to take me to work tomorrow night?"

"Ricky said you wouldn't have your car for a few weeks. I don't mind giving you rides to and from work. I know you don't want to be stuck with me, but I swear to you, I'll act like a respectable human and do my best not to make you any more uncomfortable."

I didn't understand my own feelings at the moment. I felt bad because he sounded hurt. Why should that bother me after what he had done? He didn't deserve my sympathy. The last time I gave him a chance he was a raging assmonkey.

The thing was, I wasn't the sort of person that wanted revenge. Grudges and revenge were in Maris' realm. I guess if I was being honest, there was something in me that wanted to give him another chance, I just didn't want him to prove me stupid.

Again.

I made my decision to stop being a brat and gave him a conciliatory smile. "Okay. Yeah. If you could start giving me rides, that would be helpful. I want us to be civil and friendly, but don't flirt with me. I don't want you to look at me the way you have been either. Please don't mention it to the entire school. My sister still goes there, and I don't want drama in my home, and I'm sure you're aware that she hates you. Please don't make me have to listen to her enumerate your sins."

He shook his head and tapped his fingers on the steering wheel as he looked at me. "What would I tell people, Jace?"

"I don't know, maybe getting girls in your car is your new way of getting pics of boobs. I'm not one of your girls. I won't be one, and I don't want to be talked about in the locker room or at lunch in the cafeteria. Keep my name out of your mouth. You understand me?" I said with deadly calm.

Ky's response was soft. "I know I was really a dick."

I gave a solid nod of agreement and grabbed the door handle. The front light was on, although I knew no one was home.

"I'll be here at three thirty p.m. tomorrow to pick you up. I won't tell anyone I'm giving you a ride to and from work, but Mare is going to find out. So you should probably warn her before she sees me pull into the driveway, and there is World War III and a car bombing in your driveway." He gave a weak smile.

"Just remember your promise to be friendly and not a jackass, and we'll be fine," I reminded him, opening the door and getting out without looking back.

Before I closed it, he said, "I'm going to prove to you, I'm someone worth knowing."

I ignored him and headed up to the house and unlocked the door. He didn't pull away, and I opened the door and let myself in. I leaned against it and closed my eyes once inside, whispering to myself. "Do not mistake jackasses for good guys, Jacelyn."

eight

. . .

I HAPPENED to be up early Monday morning. I wanted to make Maris breakfast before she left for school. I considered it one of my tasks in the house to help my mom out. It grossed me out to make meat and eggs for the two of them, but not everyone is vegetarian and I was already getting desensitized to it at work.

While she munched on French toast and bacon, I decided to take Ky's advice and drop the news. I watched her head figuratively explode into a million angry pieces of Mare-shrapnel.

"Jace, you aren't serious. Tell me you aren't serious! Why?" she ranted. "Wasn't he a big enough jackass to you before? Why do you feel the need to hang out with him again? You want to show him your tits now? Really?"

I knew it wouldn't be a pleasant conversation, and I hated the idea of having it. The insinuation that I was a stupid waif, really pissed me off. Maris always went off the rails, it was her defining trait, so I tried not to be defensive or reactive. After all, somewhere underneath the insults, she was trying to look out for me.

"I'm not *hanging out* with him, Mare. I'm getting rides *to* and *from* work from him while we wait for the Bug to get here. Don't make this out to be a mountain when it's nothing at all." I flipped another piece of French toast because she could eat enough to feed an army.

The frustration and concern came off her in waves. She chewed like the food could be punished for my transgressions, which meant her mouth opened and closed like she was a barn animal. Finally, she shrugged, clearly angry. "I guess you know what you're doing. You're a high school graduate after all. Just don't fall for his line of shit again. You're worth more than that."

She was so passive aggressive, it wasn't funny.

I was quiet while I grabbed Just Egg from the fridge to make myself scrambled eggs on toast. I glanced at my sister. "Is he still like he was in sophomore year?" I asked quietly.

He swore he wasn't, but he's got a horse in the race, so he'd say anything to try to convince me he was better than he once was. I was wondering if anyone would corroborate this change.

"Well last year, his sister started high school and the guys on the football team he's on, made some comments about her. Heath Morgan tried to get her to sleep with him at one of Laney Mercer's parties. Ky went a little crazy. He went through a reformation and started seeing Shea Reilly seriously. She wasn't that serious about him though and cheated on him *all* the time. I never heard a word about him stepping out on her though. Still changes nothing in my opinion—once a dog, always a dog. I don't care how he acts now, it won't wash away the past." She looked hurt as she said the last bit.

I don't think she was talking about Ky, I think she was

talking about our dad, but that was a can of worms I didn't want to open right now. We both had a long day before us.

"I don't know, he's good to his sister, Jacelyn. But he wasn't good to mine. That is all that matters to me," she added.

I tried not to show my sister that what she was saying meant something to me. It made me more curious about him, which I knew was bad news. "What's his sister like?"

"She's a lot like you. Sophie's nice, she's grounded. I've never seen her buy into the popular crap that Ky gave into. Now, their younger brother is in ninth grade. The three of them spend a good deal of time together. I guess you could say Ky protects them. He eats lunch with them instead of at the jock table. He hasn't dated anyone this year, just hung out with his family–which is kinda weird now that I think about it. Sophie's entire posse wants to bag the great Ky Linley. I don't know if they are even truly there for her."

"Sophie's his sister? What's his brother's name?" I felt like I should know this. I thought I knew everything about him from growing up with him, but I now realized that everything I knew was superficial stuff, like his locker, jersey number and the colors of his eyes. I spent so much time looking at him growing up, I never talked to him until that fateful few weeks in ninth grade, and he was playing with me the entire time. He never told me anything about himself.

"Yeah, Sophie is his sister. Taylor is his brother. Taylor is kind of weird. He's really quiet, always trying to avoid any attention. I feel bad for him a lot of the time. He's kind of cute, one day he'll be hot, but he doesn't really know how to handle girls who come up to him to get on his radar. He's the exact opposite of Ky." Maris stood and moved to the sink and dumped her dishes in. I looked at them and didn't say anything. I guess I was doing dishes at home too.

A horn honked. Mare bounced to the window and looked out. She smiled over her shoulder. "Alex is here. Thanks for breakfast. See you tonight."

I nodded and waved weakly at her receding back as she rushed out the door to her ride. The house was quiet once she was gone. Mom was sleeping and wouldn't be awake before noon. I had hours to kill, and now I didn't have homework to do or a car to use. Getting comfy on the couch, I grabbed my mom's iPad and started scoping out her book selection. It was a lot different than mine. I found a Dean Koontz book and kicked back.

"Hey, baby?" My mom shook my shoulder, and I jumped and her iPad thumped to the carpeted floor. I rubbed my eyes. "Jacie, I told you not to worry about getting a job. We're fine. You're exhausted, and you only just got home. We can make it on my paycheck. I appreciate it, but you don't have to do this."

"I'm not exhausted, I'm a little tired because I got up to talk to Mare this morning. I made her breakfast too–crap, I left dishes everywhere. Sorry mom." I facepalm. Here I was trying to make her life easier, and I made chores for her.

She laughed. "This is your first summer since you left and aren't doing homework. You should enjoy it. You are done taking care of your dad, you don't have to take care of us. Your job is to go out and screw up, make me worry, come home late from partying and make questionable choices," she joked.

"You want two Marises?" I smiled.

"I worry. I don't want you to feel you have to work in an Italian Restaurant, feed your family, and take care of your older sister. I'm the mom. It's okay to be irresponsible. You deserve it. You've been very disciplined since you left." I sighed and nodded. Oddly, I responded to that by getting up and going and making my mom a coffee. She liked the instant type, with so much sugar it would give an elephant cavities, and enough milk to turn it white.

"What are you doing, hon?" she asked, watching me.

"We're having a grown up conversation, and you sound a little unbalanced, I'm getting you coffee," I teased. I stirred the creamer and brought it to the table and sat it down so she'd get the idea that she should relax. "I want to work. It's boring doing nothing. Plus, I have plenty of time to get up to trouble that will give you graying hair. It doesn't take a lot of effort to get pregnant, and I can always get someone to buy me alcohol to start an early drinking problem. If something like that would make you happy, I can try either option for you," I say facetiously.

"I would prefer irresponsible drinking without the long term habit. I'm not ready to be a grandmother. Although, I have no doubt, if it happened, you'd step up and handle it better than I did when it happened, and I was an adult when I had Maris. You're just so put together. I wish you were selfish like your father and Mare. At least I can count on her being useless to me all summer. And I have no use for your dad at all. You're my golden child, Jacelyn."

"I'll find a bad crowd and start making friends with questionable characters immediately just for you, mom," I teased. "Maybe find a guy with a one word name... Rancid? He will ride a motorcycle and not wash." I moved to the fridge and pulled out the sweet tea I made and poured a tall glass and took a long drink before pouring more and continued. "I'll shave my head into a mohawk, dye it green and put a hole through my cheek."

My mother smiled broadly, liking this game. "See? Now we're talking. You'll have your thing, and Mare will have avoiding reality and things at home, and driving badly. I'm sad now that I didn't have a son to sneak around with a girl from the wrong side of the tracks, but you and Rancid should have that covered."

I moved to the table and sat on one leg folded beneath me and pointed at her. "You have Peter, and he is dating a boy who is on the wrong side of the closet door."

She waved her head and lifted her cup for a sip, "He's just one of my girls. I guess I can consider him the daughter sneaking around though."

I loved my mom. She was just one of those people who tried to find the humor in everything. We often had conversations that were ridiculous like this. She told me that her favorite thing was to hear us laugh, and her second favorite thing was to have something to laugh about. The way her mind worked always made me feel better, lighter. My mom put me at ease about serious things.

I know Maris took her for granted, but having spent two years with my dad, I appreciated her in a way I never would have had I stayed here. The time apart gave us both a different view of one another.

She wasn't just my mom, she was one of my best friends.

"I've heard everything you said. I want you to know I like working. I don't like having all this spare time to sit and kill. It's boring. I also like the people I work with. It's healthy, and next week when I get paid, I'd like to take over buying some of the groceries, at least my own." I held up my hand when she looked like she was going to argue. "I know you can afford it, but I'm going to have to start affording my own things this fall. I'm going to put the rest away for college."

"Jesus, Jacelyn, you're killing me!" my mom moaned. "Very well. So independent. What are your hours?"

"I'm part-time until I get my car, and then I'll be full-time," I replied.

She nodded. "How are you getting to work in the time being? I feel awful that I never got a second car now."

I saw the lines on her face and reached across the table and tapped the surface. "We are fine. A guy from work is getting me to and from work. Ricky put us on the same shifts so there wouldn't be any conflicts. I–" I sighed. "Peter stranded me for a date the other night."

She made a face and nodded in a way that said it's to be expected. "It's good you have a reliable ride then. Do I need to worry that he's some thirty-year old pedofile? Or worse a twenty something hottie who sells sex to uptight, responsible types?"

I laugh. "Closer on number two, but no cigar. It's Ky Linley. Maris has already had a fit, so you can relax. He's a teenage heartbreaker, who I remember well enough, makes fools of young girls. I know his flirting doesn't mean he likes me."

"Jacelyn," my mom's tone is one of understanding. "Just so you know, boys grow up. It's not all G.I. Joe's and girls' panties forever. Don't discount him just because of something he did when he was a kid. He could surprise you."

"It was my bra he wanted to see, not my panties," I say dryly.

"His dad had a spell where he came into the bar for a little while. The Linleys were going through something really difficult as a family. I don't want to divulge something that is personal and not mine to tell, but it changes a person, and Carter said the entire family was rethinking their actions." She looked contemplative.

"Do you think dad could change?" I asked quietly.

"I think he did once. He could again, but I changed too, if you're asking if we could ever go back. There's no chance." Her contemplation now looked regretful.

I got up and went around and hugged her. "You'd be horrible together now. He's like Mare in every way, it's why she can't stand him or forgive him. Between you and me, you'll do better with her too when she leaves the house."

"I don't hate living with your sister," she said.

"I'm not saying you do." I kissed her cheek. "But you won't have to kill yourself to keep going when you don't have to live for two people."

She patted my arm. "I have some errands to run before I have to come back here and get ready for work. What time are you leaving?"

"I'm getting picked up at three-thirty." I let her stand and hugged her tightly.

"I have to work at four too. Take a shower early, Jace, so there will be hot water for me?" She raised an eyebrow.

I nodded. "I'll shower this afternoon, do the dishes and cook you and Mare something for dinner and leave it, so all you have to do is warm it."

Her smile meant everything to me, I knew I was helping her and if I could relieve even a little of her stress, it was something.

nine

. . .

RICKY GREETED me as I came in ahead of Ky on the following Saturday. "Great, now that you are here, I'd like to meet one of the new waitresses, you should know everyone. I want you to know who might come back to ask questions in the kitchen. Then, Jacelyn, can you get some desserts in the display cooler out in the dining room. I have a front room shirt for you in the back. If you stay a few more weeks, you will get some more tees and button-downs."

The night went by quickly. It was busy, and I got my seven o'clock break at eight-fifteen. I stepped out of the back door with a slice of pizza to get some fresh air and almost walked into Ky, who had an oven bag in his hand and was coming back from a delivery.

"What do you think, you like it here?" He motioned with his chin at the building.

I nodded. "It's good. Not difficult and time flies on nights like tonight. How long have you been working here?"

He leaned against the rock facade of the building and relaxed. "I started here the summer of my sophomore year. My dad and Ricky are friends. I was a busboy at first, then a dishwasher... I filled in waiting some nights. Didn't start delivering until last November when our old delivery guy quit."

I watched his face. I knew I was staring again, but he was just as intent on me, so the rudeness wasn't one sided. "You do know how to do a little of everything here."

"Ricky's been calling me in to cover all the shifts for a while now. I don't mind. The money's good, and I'm saving for college. If I don't take one of those scholarships, my family has to pay out of pocket. I don't want the burden to be completely on my mom and dad's shoulders, when they are still going to have Soph and Tay to cover soon too."

I looked down and noticed his shoelace was untied but said nothing. It's just a reminder that he's far from perfect, especially during this moment when I'm softening to him because if I understood anything, it was not wanting to be a burden. I grudgingly took points from the jackass column and put them in the good guy one for him caring for his family.

"I need to get—" He lifted his arm to the door as it opened.

Melissa stuck her head out. "What are you both doing out here? Ky, get in here, Shea is at the counter giving Madison a hard time. Sorry, Jace, but I need you to come back in and get back in prep. I'll see you get another break or a longer lunch."

Shea... there was another reminder. As Ky stepped aside to hold the door for me, I started praying to myself, "God grant me the serenity to accept the things I cannot change, change the things I can, and the ability to discern some hot looking trouble from a good thing when I see it."

"You think I'm hot?" He smirked.

"No, just trouble." I shook my head and rushed by.

"I feel the same, Jacelyn," he yelled after me.

I turned around and walked backwards down the hall. "That is against the rules we made, Ky."

"You broke them first." He grinned.

"Are we in first grade?" I narrowed my eyes at him.

He sighed. "I wish I could do it all over again. We'd be sweethearts from the start."

"Shut up and go take care of your girlfriend!" I turned and pushed the doors to the kitchen open and entered Melissa Shoop-ba-dooping.

"Ummm, you're packed and you're stacked 'specially in the back. Brother, wanna thank your mother for a butt like that..." She danced to the ovens and stuck a meat-eaters pizza in the oven, and I made a face and tried not to gag. The meat thing still did nothing for me.

A couple minutes later, Ky came in. "It will break my family's heart, but I'm going to have to go into WITSEC because cray cray Shea isn't going away."

"I thought she broke up with you." Melissa turned down the radio. She was going into momma bear mode. I could tell by the look on her face, she was protective of this jackass.

He exhaled then snorted. "Jace, sorry to dump in front of you, but Mel's my therapist. You can go about your duties and ignore my whining."

Melissa cut him a piece of pizza and then after he inhaled it, she pointed to his next task. "Talk and work."

"She wanted a modern relationship... that means an open one. She wanted the title of boyfriend and girlfriend but to have the freedom to fuck around with other people. I didn't want that. I–" He looked at me with a regretful gaze. "I've made a lot of young and dumb mistakes and I want a one girl, one guy relationship. She said she was down with that, then immediately cheated."

"Is it cheating if you know the color of the leopard's spots?" I asked nosing into the conversation.

Melissa shrugs. "She's got a point. But go on."

"So I shut her down. Ever since, she's been sniffing around about getting back together. She said I'm not seeing the bigger picture, and it's only a few more weeks. It's about 'high school memories.' We can be king and queen of the senior class if I'd just fall in line. I have no interest in her, falling in line or her 'high school memories.'" Every time he said the words, he made air quotes. They must have really offended him.

He grabbed a ticket, washed his hands, snagged a wad of dough and pushed Melissa out of the way. I then watched him take his frustrations out on the pie crust. My mom in her weird lusting ways always talked about man hands and how manly hands can be sexy, and now looking at how Ky was capably working, I feared again that I would one day become my mom.

Melissa started giving him her opinion, and I listened in until Andy, our dishwasher, turned around with blood all over him. I instantly grabbed a dish towel and wrapped it around his hand and dragged him with me to Ricky's office.

"Fuck, man. Ricky. I broke a glass in the sink and didn't know until I cut my palm open. I need stitches."

Ricky stood and grabbed his keys. "Let's go." He then turned to me. "Tell the counter there are no deliveries tonight after the ones already on the tickets. There is a biohazard cleanup kit in the back to clean up the floor and the sink with. Melissa and Ky are in charge. Tell Melissa to make the bank drop. Do *not* tell her that in front of anyone other than Ky."

I nodded.

When I got back to the kitchen, Ky was already cleaning up the area that had been contaminated with blood. Melissa smiled at me. "Quick thinking and calm as a lullaby. You did a good job."

I moved to her side. "Ricky said you are to do the cash drop tonight, and you and Ky are in charge."

She nodded. "Bastard. I'm going to miss my friends and get there close to closing time."

Ky came over. "Cash drop?"

Melissa nodded.

"We can do it." He nodded back to the sink. "We can't use the sink for twelve hours."

"What about the dishwasher?" I pointed to the huge rack.

"It's going to handle all the plates, glasses and utensils but not the pots, pans or stuff Rick's morning crew will hate us for." Ky grinned.

There was something about that grin. My butterflies were back for no reason. I'd been working beside him and talking with him all night, there was no reason for the way my stomach fluttered. I looked up into his eyes, and they were more blue than gray at the moment. It took my breath away.

I stepped back and turned around. Under my breath I reminded myself, "Down girl, Just because his eyes are deep and soulful, doesn't mean you know what kind of waters those are, and you really can't jump into them. They could very well drown you."

With that pep talk, I went back to work and finished my shift for the night as food prep and dishwasher.

Ky had to do the last two deliveries we already had tickets for when they stopped taking them, and I didn't see him again until midway through our closeup duties. He walked in and did a hand off with Melissa that I suspected was the cash from the till. They let the waitresses and hostess go, leaving the busboy who was cleaning the floor and the three of us. Luckily, it wasn't Artie. I couldn't deal with handsy Artie tonight. I was getting more and more worked up as the night went on about my ride home.

Josh let us know he had to do the bathrooms, and I moved to do the windows in the front.

"Jace, take a break. It's been a stressful night. You already earned your hourly," Melissa said.

I looked at her then at Ky nervously. I was using her as a human shield, and by the agitation in his shoulders and face, he knew.

When Josh came out, he and Melissa headed to the front door to let themselves out while Ky went to the back to get the cash drop. I was looking outside when I heard a noise behind me and turned to find him gazing at me intently. His eyes were taking in my body in my skinny jeans and t-shirt. Ky wasn't leering, but he was definitely checking me out.

I felt a flutter in my stomach, and my breath sped up. I looked back outside for a moment and then took a deep breath before turning back to him. His lips twitched, and he smiled. I felt the same dumb giddiness I felt in the start of freshman year when he walked by me, and I caught his eye.

"You're stupidly good looking, Ky." I sighed. "I just can't afford to be dumb again."

He started laughing and nodded. "You're really beautiful and before you get suspicious, that's not a line. We're ready to go when you're done staring out at the parking lot."

I nodded. He handed me the cash bag and had me unlock the door before he went to the alarm system and set it. There were two doors, the inner door which he locked first then pushed me out the other before locking it. "Woohoo. We only have thirty seconds to get out and lock both doors. I would have had you wait outside, but I didn't feel safe doing that."

"Well, no. I had the cash." I patted the bag and looked around as we made our way to the car.

"No, Jacelyn. You're more precious than the cash." He opened the door and shook his head like I was the dork.

When he got in, he apologized. "The bank is one town over. We have to go there first. The one across the street doesn't have a night drop."

"Small town charm." I laughed.

"Do that again. Wait, that never works. It's just... I hate how tied up in knots and stressed out you are when we are together. Your laugh is really great." He was smiling again.

Could I both love and hate a smile?

"I really wish you were easier to be with. It sucks to be waiting for the other shoe to drop," I said, rubbing my palms on my thighs.

"Would you rather have another ride to work? Josh could probably help out a few days a week. Or, if you weren't freaked out, I know someone who could. She just turned sixteen, but she's a decent driver."

"It's fine. You don't need to get a girlfriend to drive me. I shouldn't be so ridiculous." I tried really hard to give my most sincere smile. I wondered if it was apparent how fake I was being in the face of him having a girlfriend.

"I don't, Jace." He shook his head.

"Don't what?" I whispered.

He started the car, and it rumbled. "I don't have a girlfriend. I have a sister, who has a cute little hand me down Fiat from our grandma. She could give you a ride."

I closed my eyes and hung my head. "I'm so sorry. I'm so confused. Even after what you said tonight... Maris told me the other day that you and Shea are on again and off again. I don't want to be part of drama or games."

"Shea and I were seeing one another. But like I said today, only one of us was serious about that, and it was a one-sided relationship. I know this probably doesn't make sense, but she has a lot going on at home, and I would love to be a friend to her and help her, but she's..." He started to laugh. "I don't have a nice way to say 'bat-shit crazy.'"

We hadn't left the parking lot yet, the two of us were just sitting there. "Are you seeing anyone? I saw you at Jimmy's with Alex's brother, Trick. Do you have something going on with him?"

I laughed at the outrageousness of that. "Trick? Yeah. My sister and her hope for a happy match. No. I have nothing going on with him. I only met him that night and he was... on the make. I'm not into him at all. Mare would love for me to fall in line, so we could do couples stuff with her and Alex, but that isn't going to fly. I'm actually hoping he found Rosa interesting enough to lose my number."

Ky's bit his lower lip and grinned. I wasn't imagining things. He was really excited I wasn't dating anyone.

I gave myself a mental shake. This was the boy who shattered my heart and humiliated me, and here I sat, trying to decipher his thoughts like I was still that same school girl.

I never realized I was the type of person who sought out my own destruction until Ky Linley came back into my life, but I really seemed to be courting disaster.

"We should do that drop." I nod to the money in my lap.

"Have you taken a look around town yet? A lot of things have changed." He put the car into gear, and then softly put on the radio. It was old school, and he turned it to the classic rock channel. "This is an awesome song. "Wish You Were Here" by Pink Floyd."

I started to laugh. "You're... What do they call them in that S.E. Hinton book? A Greaser!"

He looked at me and smiled. "Yeah, a cliché, I drive a muscle car and listen to classic rock. My dad got me listening to it when we were rebuilding it. He rebuilt his with his dad, and they listened to the same stuff and bonded the same way." He pointed and slowed down. "Look, Hershey's Deli is gone, and there's a Taco Bell there now."

Hershey's was a hoagie shop that Maris and I went to with dad on our 'Daddy/Daughter days.' Maris probably helped Taco Bell heave them out of business to wipe another memory of dad from this place, I thought bitterly.

I finally murmured answering Ky, "I haven't been around Fellsdale or Lake Alto since I came back. Peter took me to the mall when I was job hunting in Maystown. But he didn't give me a tour of town. He's been really busy lately."

"Yeah, he has!" Ky smirked.

"What does that mean?" I asked.

"Do I know something you don't know?" Ky teased. "I'll make a deal with you. We do this drop, which is coming up right at the next strip mall, and you let me show you Fellsdale and Lake Alto–I'm not trying to get you in my back-seat, I swear on my family's well being. It's twelve fifty now. I'll have you home by two a.m. at the latest, and I'll tell you what I know about Peter."

Would it really hurt to prolong my time with Ky? I badly wanted to. Without giving myself a chance to start the pro and con debate, I nodded. "Sure, but you screw this up, and you don't get any more chances."

He grinned and pulled into the bank and rounded to the back side. Before he got out near the bankdrop, he held out his hand to shake. "And if I ace this, you give me another shot at going out."

I looked at his hand, and nodded again before shaking his hand to seal the deal.

He laughed happily and got out of the car, leaving the door open.

Getting back in, he swung the car around and stopped at the sign. "Wait, I should do this right. You have radio privs."

"Can you get the College Radio station on here?" I asked.

"Try it." He was still smiling happily as I swung the buttons until I reached WMAY and "Bad Life" by Sigrid and Bring Me The Horizon came on.

His face grimaced a little, and I laughed. "You said I could choose, and this is awesome. Show me the world Jeeves."

He pulled out and headed to Lake Alto. Marcie Carlton's dad opened a collectables shop by the junior high. I never thought it would survive the first six months, but Marcie says it's doing really well. Her dad sunk everything in it though. He has everything from baseball cards to Beanie Babies there. I bought my brother a 12" Luke Skywalker collectible doll from the 90's there for his last birthday.

"Mare said you spend a lot of time with your brother and sister at school. Don't your friends miss you? Don't they think it's weird?" I searched.

His face tightened, and his hands on the steering wheel slid a little. He shook his head and looked over at me. "My mom was diagnosed with breast cancer the summer before my junior year... HER-2 positive. Stage 2, metastatic. It was scary for all of us. You know, you can get mad and hate the world, or you can come together. I had to come together because I had Soph and Taylor, and they had no idea what was going on or what to do. It straightened out my priorities. So, do I care what people at school think about how tight we are? Not at all. Do they miss me? If they do, it's not one iota of what it would be if I lost my mom. I'm not going to pick them over family."

"Wow," I said, not knowing what else to say. I felt some of the asshole veneer chip off of Ky's image. "I don't think you would have said that when we were talking at the start of my freshman year. You always wanted to be the center of things."

"You have to understand, Jace. My mom is the best. She's just incredible, strong and smart. When she got sick, I had this realization that I wasn't someone that my mom could be proud of, she was sick and here I was a dumb fucker collecting notches on my bed post. It slammed into me like a truck, how easy it was to have my family threatened. All those people at school, and all that bullshit, was suddenly unimportant.

"I realized I didn't care who liked me for the next two years at school, if it meant that I would be spending every Mother's Day putting flowers on her grave. I shrugged off a lot of people, so I could pull the ones that were important closer."

We pulled into a church parking lot, and I noticed that the back of it, where there used to be four houses, was cleared and replaced with a pavilion.

I watched Ky closely as he took off his baseball cap and tossed it in the backseat and ran his hands in his hair. My eyes skimmed his features. He looked the same as he did earlier tonight but somehow better now. I was trying to fit all these new puzzle pieces together.

"I'd like to meet them," I said it outloud before I had a chance to stop myself.

His smile was genuine and nodded. "I think that's an excellent idea. I know I'm bragging, but my brother and sister are fucking awesome. Sophie could use a good friend too, and I know you are quality–no pressure."

We both laughed.

I thought about Mare. She was awesome too. What would I have done if my mom was diagnosed with some illness? She'd already been through so much, I didn't need her to be threatened to know what was important, it was clear to me already.

"I know what you mean about families being delicate and precious. After my dad divorced my mom, I realized something special had been destroyed. My mom is amazing too. My dad cheated on her, and she tries to keep positive and looking forward, never saying anything bad to us girls about him. She was so supportive and under-standing when I went to live with him, though I know it had to hurt her. I feel like I owe her now." I felt my lip tremble.

I never talked about what happened. I was surprised to hear myself divulging the darkest parts of my heart to Ky. But he'd bared his heart to me, so it felt wrong not to share something in return.

Ky nodded. "Mare became even angrier after you left. I know she's a good person, Jace. She's always had her heart in the right place. Please don't take this the wrong way, your sister became downright bitchy when you left." The look on his face revealed worry that he'd overstepped, but I got what he was saying.

"She really hates my dad. When I left, she wouldn't speak to me for three months. She couldn't understand why

I would go with someone who could cheat on his family." I swallowed and looked out the windshield.

"Why did you go?" His voice was soft and searching.

I sighed. If I told him, I would be wide open. It would give him hope. Peter had said a million times that this was my mechanic, I was a forgiver. "I didn't want him to be alone. He didn't know what he was getting into. His head was full of ideas and plans, hearts and flowers. I didn't want him hurt, even after he had annihilated us. So I went to watch over him. I know what he did was unforgivable. But he's my dad, and I care about him. There are times when you have to do the unthinkable and find the strength to do the charitable thing. My dad isn't a bad person, he's an idiot.

"Maris has no time for idiots. But the truth exists, and I see it for what it is. If my parents were truly happy, this wouldn't have happened. So this gives them both a chance to find that happiness somewhere else."

I felt sad having poured it out, not better.

"That is a really, really mature point of view on the situation. I think that I would have been more like Maris if it happened to my family. I would have held it against my dad and been angry," he said with a troubled look on his face.

"I don't know... I think you might have surprised yourself. I never had the thought in my head as to what I would do 'if' before it happened. I feel guilty for not being here to support my mom, but she's a survivor."

Ky was quiet for a few minutes after I was done speaking. "Have you always been so intuitive?"

I gave a choking laugh. "Me? Intuitive? I'm a chump."

He shook his head, inhaled and pointed at his phone. "We lost track of time. It's one-twenty, and I'm not trying to cut this short, but I'm actually tired from all this heavy talk. Maybe we can do the tour tomorrow night."

Ky was right, it was late, and I had just told a guy I didn't trust a bunch of intimate things about my life. *What was I thinking?!* Anxiety was setting in now. He stopped at the exit to the church and turned to me, picking up his phone.

"I fucked this up last time, but could I have your number? We don't work again until Thursday, and like I said, I'd like to finish this tomorrow night."

I looked down at his phone.

"I can give you mine, and you can decide later," he offered.

I took his number and input it into my phone. "I make no promises."

His lips tipped up on one side. "I feel like I won the lottery all the same."

We drove more or less in comfortable silence around Lake Alto, and I sang while "Where Is My Mind?" by Tkay Maidza played. I couldn't help but think it was my new anthem.

We were almost to my development when I remembered he was going to tell me about Peter. "So, what do you know about my friend that I don't."

Ky laughed, and it sent chills through me. "I can't say a lot because it's not my secret to tell, but my sister is best friends with the guy he's seeing. You get her on your side, and you'll meet him."

My jaw dropped. "You know the Narnia boy!" I asked.

He started laughing. "Yes, and he would love knowing he's a Narnia boy."

We pulled into my driveway and Ky took a deep breath. "About meeting Sophie and Taylor... We are all going to a movie Saturday afternoon. We do it every weekend. Would you and Peter like to come along? Mare and Alex too–although I know better."

A movie with The Linley Family. I wanted to go, I really did. The part of me that was smart and knew better than to trust Ky was oddly silent. I held up my phone. "I'll text and let you know what Peter says."

The porch light flickered on and off about ten times, and I rolled my eyes. "Great!" I exhaled. "Momma Maris and I are going to talk about me getting home so late after my non-existent curfew."

Ky got out and came around to open my car door before I had a chance to gather myself and waved goodnight. I dragged my feet up the path to the door and acted like I was unlocking the door, even though I knew it was unlocked. Ky pulled out of the driveway as I went in.

"Where the hell have you been?" Maris stood in the living room with a look of fury on her face.

"I had work. I have a job now." I tossed my bag down and crashed on the couch next to it.

"Mom told me you were getting off at twelve and it's almost two. Two hours after you got off of work. The least you could have done is called." She looked at me with narrowed eyes, cataloging my appearance. Mare seemed to be looking for signs that I removed my clothes and redressed in the night.

"Maris, I worked until one. We close at midnight. The other thing is, I don't owe you an explanation. I'm an adult, who graduated already, and has a job. I went for a ride after work. It's not a big deal."

"Were you with Linley? That cretin that uses girls like Kleenex and tosses them away when he blows his load in them?" Maris asked, vulgarly. She wasn't going to back down. I had half a mind to leave her question unanswered, but she would only get more angry. It would be better to confront her anxiety and deal with it.

"Yes, I was with Ky, and no, nothing happened. We talked. Nothing more, so get your mind out of the gutter." I patted the cushion next to me. She stared at the door a few minutes before her shoulders fell, and she came my way and joined me.

"He's not a good person, Jacelyn. Don't give him a chance to hurt you. He's just like dad but worse," she said, almost desperately.

ten

. . .

"DICE THOSE, and then throw them in the pan with the olive oil." I ordered like I was Gordon Ramsey Jr. with a flick of a wrist and a commanding tone. Peter had come over for dinner–actually, he came over to hang out and gossip, but I put him to work cutting vegetables.

He brushed at his cheeks. "Does this crying while cutting onions thing ever *not* happen?"

"That's a sweet onion, it shouldn't make you cry, you baby. Perhaps you are sympathizing with the plight of onions everywhere." I made a mocking pout.

He nodded in agreement, and dumped them into the skillet. "Oh, see there they go! I told them that life was too precious to take the leap into something that would get them burned, but did they listen? It's truly impeccable advice, I wish the person who wanted to turn them into the meal would consider the caution too!" He raised his eyebrows and sighed.

I shrugged. "Alexa, turn up volume two." "Loser" by Sueco blared.

Peter leaned over the device and raised his voice. "Alexa, play "Shoong!" by Taeyang and Lisa."

He started doing the dance, which is no doubt from the music video. I laughed. "Alexa, volume down two."

I shook my head and turned away from him to cut the chicken breast into cubes. I grimaced at the feeling in my glove covered hands. I became a vegetarian for a reason. I didn't want to touch this stuff, but my mom and sister still ate it so now, here I was.

"I'm serious, Waverly!" Peter slammed his hand down on the counter. "Don't be an onion!"

I waved his words away with a glove covered hand. It was becoming harder and harder to listen to him and Maris warning me off about Ky, meanwhile, I was seeing someone worthy at work. Their lack of faith in me was annoying and kicked in this annoying rebellion inside me that I hated.

"That chicky chicky didn't do anything to make you handle it like that," he said more gently, as I manhandled the pink flesh.

"You know what I want?" I asked with gritted teeth.

"Your car to be here? A windfall for your mom? Your sister to stop throwing Trick at you?" Peter replied all tongue in cheek.

"I really want you and Mare to stop. I'm fine. Will you come with me on Saturday or not? This isn't a date, I'm asking you to come with me, so I can meet his brother and sister because they sound like really awesome people, and I could use more of those in my life and less Tricks. I want you to come without lecturing me, if you are capable of that." I could hear that whining at the end of that sentence, and I hated it.

Peter took a bell pepper and tossed it into the air, caught it, sighed and picked up the knife. He started chunking it in a way that would make Anne Burrell cry. "Truth? I wouldn't miss it for the world. Any chance we can convince Alex and Mare to come? I like seeing public displays of violence."

I ground my teeth. "Crap on a cracker, Peter Kim! Can't you let it go? Even for me?"

"Let what go?" Maris asked as she entered the kitchen taking off her sweater.

My eyes flew to Peter's in plea. He smiled and replied. "I am in a fight to the death over the rights and liberties of onions from the corner of each nation. Jace thinks they should all fry, and God should sort them out."

My sister rolled her eyes. "I'm happy to see you two are thinking about vegetable activism. A lot of agricultural practices do keep the good greens down. Keep the gravity of important issues at the forefront of the social spectrum."

"Come on Noona, you know you love being part of our high level conservatism conversation." Peter liked calling my sister noona. It meant older sister in Korean culture. It was a term of respect, not to mention that it came with a hefty amount of affection.

"What's for dinner?" Maris asked, while peering into the pan. Peter lifted an eyebrow asking the same thing, even though he was part of the preparation.

I nodded my head toward the bottle on the counter. "We're having teriyaki chicken. I didn't have time to marinate it though."

My sister moaned in approval, and Peter made a face as we added the chicken and peppers at the same time.

"You need a wok, Jace," he grumbled.

I shrugged and yawned. "Don't have one. You are getting skillet teriyaki."

"After dinner, do you mind if I steal my sister for the

night? We need to go shopping for a gift for Alex and Trick's mom for her birthday." I looked in time to see my sister giving my friend a gesture of prayer.

"Can't Peter come with?" I asked.

Mare looked again at Peter and said, "It's going to be really boring. He won't have any fun."

"Then why do you want me to go?" I asked. "I'm exhausted."

She seemed torn, looking for another argument. I was about to call her on her bullshit when Peter held up his hands and nodded. "Actually, I have a lot of studying to do. If you don't mind, I'm going to scoot after dinner"

My sister beamed at him, and I just knew that I was going to hate whatever my sister was planning. I hated the Machiavellian plans she had. She wanted to orchestrate this relationship, and it wasn't going to happen. She looked elated at the moment though. "How long do I have before we eat? I need to take a shower."

"Twenty minutes?" I answered to her back as she was already running up the stairs.

"You know you could come with us. I don't care what she's trying to put together tonight. I care about you. I did tell her I would go with her for this shopping thing, but there is no reason you can't come too." I bumped him with my hip, so I could stir the food.

"It's not a big deal. I do have homework. You can call me tonight when you get home, and we can talk more about Saturday. I'll think about going... but I'm only considering going. I think it's going to be a catastrophe, and I think you need a friend to be there." He looked at me through sad eyes.

I was pretty sure he would come. He was suspicious of Ky, and I think he was curious too. I don't think he wanted me to go alone. I think that if he could insist on coming to work with me, he would.

It wasn't long before Maris was pushing Peter out the door and giving me a smile that told me that asking for forgiveness was easier than asking permission.

I found out why, when I slipped in the car next to Trick, and he leaned in and kissed my cheek. "Thanks for giving me a second date. I wasn't sure you would. I promise not to disappear this time."

I gave him a fake smile and glanced at my sister in the side mirror. "Oh, that's okay. I'm not really ready to date."

We wandered the mall with Trick repeatedly grabbing my hand and me liberating it, by yanking it back until my elbow was getting sore. It was kismet when we entered the engraving store and found Rosa there. Trick smiled wide for her, and Maris scowled. I couldn't help but laugh. "Mare, you can't force something that isn't there," I said quietly.

"But if you date him, we can all go out together!" she gritted out.

I shook my head. "No matter who I date, we can do that."

"Not if it's that asshat, you are hanging around with," she said in a scathing tone. She then growled and grabbed Alex's arm. "There's nothing here for her."

But I was looking at a music box that was gorgeous and on sale. "Alex, Trick!" I called them over and showed it to them. "Would your mom like this?"

Alex's smile grew slowly, and he nodded. "What would we get engraved on it?"

Trick was an eternal idiot and suggested half a dozen moronic things before Maris came out with, "How about Shakespeare? *If music be the food of love, play on.*"

I smiled at my sister, and Alex kissed her cheek.

Rosa smiled at all of us and gave Trick a coy look that the man ate up, "It will be ready on Friday."

We got in the car and Mare turned around and smacked Trick repeatedly. "What the fuck was that? You are on a date with my sister, and you are flirting with some cooch?"

I started to laugh and caught my sister's hand to protect Trick. "Knock it off, you psycho. Trick and I are destined to be friends. I think he and Rosa are cute together. Chill out."

He smiled and looked at me regretfully. "Sorry, I wasn't trying to be a dick."

"You weren't. I didn't even know this was going to be a date until I got in the car. Mare set this up behind my back. She's at fault for what went down. Do you have Rosa's number, or do you need it?" I offered.

He looked embarrassed. "I have it."

"Alright then." I grinned.

Mare wasn't happy though, and when we got back to the house, she insisted everyone come in to watch a movie.

"I'm really tired." I tried to excuse myself.

She turned on me like a banshee and with eyes glowing from some angry possession said, "You *will* watch this movie with us."

My shoulders slumped, and Alex gave me a commiserating look. He mouthed, '*It'll be okay,*' and I wanted to trust him, but my sister was acting like a spoiled bitch.

She left us all sitting in awkward silence, which Trick tried to fill after a few moments. "Maris said that you got a job at Piero's. That was quick, you weren't even home for two weeks. Your sister hasn't even talked about getting a job, and she's lived here eighteen years."

I don't like the comparison, it felt wrong. "Yeah, well I'm not going to school, and my mom needs the help. I'm sure Maris will help when she can."

Trick and Alex shared a disbelieving smirk at that. I understand why, but it seemed disloyal to allow it.

"Mare has a lot going on," I said.

Trick nodded. "Piero's has some really good food. I like the calamari. They have great cocktail sauce."

I blinked at him trying to bite my tongue. The lobster and calamari were some of the most expensive things on the menu. Should I be surprised that the Arotini's would get the top tier items? Here we are, barely scraping by, and they probably leave half the food on their plates.

I knew my reaction to his comment was assumptive and childish, but I couldn't help myself from saying, "I usually get the rigatoni marinara, it's something I can afford."

Alex must have sensed danger because he joined the conversation, saying, "They have the best meat eater's pizza. Maybe we can come by sometime when you are working and say 'hi.'"

"Ricky doesn't like employees taking personal time when they are on the clock. I wouldn't be able to say more than 'hey' before I had to go back to work. It would be pointless." I didn't mention that they can come during my lunch break and hang out.

Maris came back into the room with her arms full. I jumped up to help her. "I hope you don't mind buttered popcorn, do you? We seem to be out of the natural flavor. Jace, I brought you ice tea with enough Splenda to give you cancer in ten years." She talked fast and tried to cover her nervousness.

My exhaustion made me less and less social, and the three of them chatted while I sat quietly, in revolt of having to spend more time with Trick after having established that neither of us was into each other. Alex suggested the six of us go out this Saturday to the lake, Trick and Rosa, Peter and me, Maris and him.

Maris smiled broadly. "YES! I love Lake Alto this time of year."

"You can't even go in it yet!" I said brattily. "It's cold and stinks."

She looked like I kicked her puppy. "We can go out on Alex and Trick's boat and spend the day on the water, though."

"Can't. I'm sorry. I'm going out with friends to a movie," I said, hoping he wouldn't let me down.

"Peter can come with us, Jace," Alex offered.

I sighed. "I'm not only going out with Peter, a bunch of us are going out."

A look of irritation flashed across Maris' face, a smile quickly hid it though. "Since when do you have a group of friends? You haven't been home that long. Plus, you aren't that good at making friends."

I raised my eyebrows at her bitchiness. I didn't want to do this in front of Alex and Trick. "We can talk about it later."

"Well, maybe we can go out to the movies with you. Will your friends mind?" she asked.

"No, they won't. But we should discuss this later. Please," I begged.

"What's the big deal? Who are you hanging out with that you don't want to talk about it now?" She tilted her head and dug in more.

I sighed and gave in. There was no hope for it. She was a dog with a bone, and about to have babies over what I was going to tell her. "Peter and I are going out with Taylor, Sophie and Ky. You are more than welcome to come, all of you. Trick and Rosa, you and Alex. But you won't want to."

I saw Alex stiffen. He used to be best friends with Ky, and I didn't understand what happened between them that made him suddenly choose sides. He did know Maris' feelings about Ky though, and right now, I think he was just fortifying himself for her detonation.

"You are not!" Her tone brokered no argument.

I rolled my eyes and had no interest in her dictates. "Yes, Maris. I'm going out with the Linleys. I don't think you want to have this conversation in front of your boyfriend and his brother, so maybe you want to save it until later. I will talk about it with you in the morning."

I got up and headed upstairs before she could argue.

Trick however stood before I reached the top. "I think we should go. I'll see you tomorrow, Mare. I'm heading out. See you, Saturday, maybe, Jacelyn."

I didn't listen to Alex and Mare say goodnight.

My door was flung open and an irate Maris stood there like the figurehead of a ship warning me of an oncoming collision with a great object. "Jacelyn Beth Waverly, you are not going anywhere with Ky on Saturday. It's stupid. Why would you be so dumb?"

"Mare, knock it off. You've foisted Trick on me twice in as many weeks, and you need to leave it alone. I don't like him. He's pretentious. And, not to mention... I just don't like him, he's too old, too experienced, and started off our courtship with the worst pick-up line ever—I'm a Libra. Well I'm a stop sign!" I growled, ripping off my sweatshirt.

She plopped down on the end of my bed and ignored the fact that I was getting dressed for bed. "He's a really good guy. You haven't given him a chance. You're a grown up now, why can't you go for an adult? Someone who won't drag you through the gutter?"

"He likes Rosa!" I yelled at her. "I also don't need you to

bring home guys for me to make arranged marriages. It's not like I'm jumping into bed with Ky! We work together, and he has treated me with respect while we work, but it's nothing more. He told me about his sister, who sounds like a good person, and I want to meet her! This isn't your business!"

"This isn't my business?" she sounded hurt. "You know, maybe more of dad rubbed off on you than I thought. He didn't know what was good for him or this family either!" She got up and marched towards my door. She turned around, heartbreak in her eyes, before heading out and slamming the door behind her.

It didn't feel good upsetting her. Still, she was treating me like a little girl, and was too concerned with arranging my life since I came back. I wasn't a ninth grader anymore. I was old enough to choose my friends.

I grabbed my earpods and popped them in and hit my playlist, I was too pissed off to sleep. I hit play and listened to Mae Stephens' "If We Ever Broke Up."

eleven

. . .

"MAKE TWO CEASAR CHICKEN SALADS,
and then start filling the condiments," Melissa said. She
wasn't in that great of a mood today, and I didn't want to
irritate her further, so I nodded to her bidding without
comment.

I hadn't gotten a ride with Ky. He had texted that he
would be late and asked if I could arrange something to get
to work. Peter was on the phone with me at the time and
came to get me but apologized because he couldn't give me
a ride home. Ky was still MIA, and I wasn't sure if he
regretted talking to me Sunday night, or if I was being
narcissistic.

It was eight o'clock when Ricky yelled in the kitchen,
"Mel, take your dinner. Ky's coming in to cover you."

I waited him to come in and when he did, he
wouldn't meet my eye. He would barely look at me at all.
After a couple minutes of awkward silence went by, I
moved closer to him and tugged the back of his shirt. "Hey,"
I said. "Did I do something?"

His shoulders tensed for a moment and sighed. He

looked over his shoulder, his eyes ran over my face. Ky seemed genuinely torn about something, and I wasn't sure if I should back off or offer to listen. I sucked on my lips, and he watched and exhaled. "Your sister paid me a visit today. She seems to believe in a theory that says if you yell loud enough the message will have more meaning."

My stomach dropped to my feet. I should have known Maris would go after Ky when I failed to register her complaints. "I'm sorry. I told her to mind her own business." I knew I should say more, but I had nothing.

He shrugged his shoulders. "You know... I knew she wouldn't be happy. I didn't think she would be that angry. She was ranting about you not being dumb and being worth more. The thing was, I couldn't argue with her. I agree with her, Jacelyn."

I moved to the fridge, and started pulling out the gallon bottles of condiments then the table ones to refill. "It's not her business, Ky. I told her that last night. I would like to meet Taylor and Sophie. It's not like you're trying to trap me into something shady. This isn't a date, and it's not going to end with us in your muscle car on a remote road with me losing my virginity."

He shook his head with a self-deprecating smile and tossed a pepperoni onto the pizza with more force. He then scooped it up with a long handled pizza peel. "I'm not trying to pull something over on you. Fuck! Even in tenth grade, despite what I acted like and what I might have thought I was going to get out of you, I liked you. I was crazy for you. I may have been incredibly stupid about how to treat a girl you are crazy about, but I really wanted us to end up together. I was beyond disappointed when it all crashed and burned. Not to mention hurt that I lost Maris' friendship. I had been friends with her forever, and it sucked losing that."

Ky closed his eyes, and it gave me a moment to gather my own endless nerves. I could feel the blood that flooded my cheeks as he admitted to liking me, it wasn't a game. It hurt hearing it.

"You know the saddest part, Jacelyn? If everything had just played out back then, the rumors might have been there, but we'd have been together, and I never would have pressured you. I had a big mouth, but I wanted you more than I wanted sex. But your sister just blew things up when she found out, and she should have. She did the right thing." He looked out the window of the kitchen and seemed to be looking back through time and hating what he saw. "Anyway... When I saw you again, you were more beautiful than before. You have the greatest smile."

He stopped, looked at me and blushed a little and grabbed another wad of dough and started working it for the next order. "I don't know, Jace. It was like seeing you for the first time all over again. I had the same stupid hope I had in tenth grade. I don't want to take you out on a date on Saturday that will end with you in the back of my muscle car losing your virginity. I just want more time with you."

Pterodactyls had taken the place of the butterflies in my stomach. I was afraid there was a chance that I could possibly throw up on my own sneakers with excitement. I wondered if I was dreaming. Ky Linley—lifelong crush of mine, was baring his heart, and it was that he wanted me?

I had to be hallucinating.

"But, the thing is, your sister reminded me today at lunch, that everything I touch turns to meaningless shit. I don't want that to be you in this case. I don't think I'll ever be able to convince her differently. Hell, I don't know if I can convince myself. I think you're worth more than you could ever guess, Jacelyn–but I'm not. I'm definitely not worth making two sisters, who need one another, to fight. As much as I want you, and I do-" He looked sad. "I couldn't stomach the idea of coming between you and Mare."

"Well... I appreciate you and Maris looking out for me," I said angrily. "But neither of you determine who I make friends with. I get to choose who and what I fight for, not either of you. What really irritates me, is that no one seems to think I'm smart enough to make up my own mind." I accidentally over squeezed the ketchup into the refill bottle and caused a mess. "If you don't want me to come out with you and your family on Saturday, say that, don't dress it up as something you are doing for my own good."

Ky looked at me for a long time before shaking his head and moving away to rotate the pizzas in the oven with the pizza peel. "Damn." He looked at his hand like he burned it and sighed.

After that, he didn't say anything else and when Melissa came back in, she was in a better mood. She turned up the music and immediately started singing, "Party-people! Yeah, Tag Team music in full effect! That's me - DC the Brain Supreme, and my man Steve Roll'n! We're kickin' the flow!.."

I started laughing, and when it got to the hook, I bounced up and down. "Whoomp, there it is!"

At ten-thirty, Ky came back into the kitchen from making a delivery as I made sure the morning shift had the ingredients to make sauces.

"Do you need a ride home?" he asked quietly, like he was trying to make amends.

I shrugged. "I don't want to put you out–"

"I would really like to take you, Jace." He smiled, something still sad hung about his aura.

I raced through clean-up and closing procedures, and when Ricky told me I was free to go, I was buzzing with anticipation. Ky hardly worked in the kitchen at all tonight. He did deliveries and covered Madison, who called out at the last minute.

As usual, Ky opened his car door and as he walked back around, I leaned over to unlock his side to return the favor. He seemed a little unsure of himself when he first got in, and I didn't want him to be the nervous one just because Mare went at him at school. "How about that tour of town you offered me the other night?"

He tried to stop the grin that lit up his face from forming. "I don't know. Maris might be waiting for you, is it a good idea?"

"My mom works until two a.m., and she's the only one I need to explain myself to. I'd really like to see what has happened to Fellsdale while I was away." I smiled.

Ky sat looking out the windshield a few moments then nodded. He turned the car on and laughed when "Surrender" started playing. "This is your anthem."

"Who is this?" I asked. "Better yet, what is this?"

"Cheap Trick. Listen." He adjusted the volume and pulled out. When the chorus came on, he sang loudly and laughed. "Mommy's alright, Daddy's alright. They just seem a little weird. Surrender, surrender. But don't give yourself away..."

I leaned over and smacked him on the shoulder and turned down the song. "You're a nut. That's not my anthem. My anthem is... "The Muppets." I started to hum the theme song. Then I belted out, "It's time to play the music. It's time to light the lights. It's time to meet the Muppets on the Muppet Show tonight..."

He shook his head and chuckled. "Great, that will be stuck in my head for days."

Ky pulled into a farming supply store that had opened in the place of a closed down chain grocery store location. Oddly enough, at the other end of the same strip mall, another grocery store had opened. "The Weis is doing well, but the one that was here tanked," he explained.

I felt like a cheat. I've been here twice in the last week to buy things for making dinner. I kept my mouth shut though because we were both in a good mood, and I didn't want to do anything to spoil it.

"So, can I come to the movies with you on Saturday, or do I have to seek out an invite from your brother or sister?" I teased.

He tried not to grin but failed. "Do you really want to? I'm worried about you and your sister fighting." He sobered up, and I didn't want that to happen, I wanted to keep the vibe light and fun.

"Well, I mean... if it will make you feel better Peter agreed to go. He and I can go with your brother and sister, and you can sit in the car with the window rolled down a little." I bit my bottom lip to stop myself from laughing.

We were parked under a streetlamp in the lot, and he watched my mouth then shook his head. "Do you still feel like you need a buffer?"

I thought about it for a moment and tilted my head his way. "Actually, no, I don't. But I just got back, and I work a lot when Peter is free. I would really like to be able to do things that he can be included in. I miss him, if truth be told."

Ky smiled. "If truth be told?"

"Yeah, if truth be told. You got a problem with that?" I said with some sass.

"It's cute." He put the car in gear and started driving toward the exit. "Should I get Soph to invite the guy he likes, so he has a date?"

I arched an eyebrow, something I spent a lot of time practicing. "Why? Is this a date you are inviting me to?"

He was silent as we pulled onto the street. It was hard to see in the street lights and flashing headlights what was going on in his eyes, but it did look like his face might have turned a little red. Finally, he said, "I don't know how to answer that."

I didn't want to make him more uncomfortable, and it was enough for me that he hadn't said no. I leaned forward and fiddled with the radio station knobs until I got to the college station again. "Meet Me At Our Spot" was played by The Anxiety, Willow and Tyler Cole. "I love this song. Los Angeles is only like two and a half hours north of San Diego. I went with my friend Javier to Venice Beach and Santa Monica for a huge Memorial Beach Block Party thing that happens. There are DJs, food, games and all kinds of things. This song reminds me of that."

"This song reminds you of a guy named Javier?" Ky side-eyed me and his jaw twitched a little. "Is it like a romantic reminder?"

I smiled and then sucked on my lips. "He was a boything, but this song reminds me of the Block Party, not him."

"So, he wasn't memorable?" he asked.

I grinned. "I haven't talked to Javi in over eight months. No hard feelings or anything. It just wasn't anything either of us were into."

Ky nodded, but said nothing.

We were on the other side of town from the direction of where I lived, and it was getting late. I was having fun and really wanted to spend more time with Ky, but he had school in the morning and needed to get home.

"I should probably be getting home. It's getting late, and you have an early morning. Do you still play sports?" I asked.

"Not this season. I played football last fall. I didn't want to play baseball again though. I was okay taking it easy and just being with Sophie and Taylor this semester. I have a disc golf course in the field behind my house though. Put it up two years ago. Sometimes I still have people come over to play it. Maybe you can come over and play with us?"

"What in the world is disc golf?" I wrinkled my nose.

"Disc golf is also known as frisbee golf. It's a lot of fun." He smiled.

I said nothing, but for a few minutes, I just stared at him, then I giggled and tried to stop, which made me giggle more. I covered my mouth. "Sorry. This is all so weird and strange."

"Strange, how?" Ky asked, giving me a look like I had a few screws loose.

"I just never guessed I'd find myself here, with you. I'm having a good time. I don't know what disc golf or frisbee golf is, but you are asking me on another date, and we haven't established if you asked me on the first one yet! It's all very weird. If you just knew how much five year old me wanted to marry six year old you, you'd run now."

"Well if that isn't a red flag, nothing is, but I have some scary facts about seven or eight year old me, so I won't run too far away. I have a half-day of school tomorrow. If you would like, maybe we could go get something to eat before we go to work." His lips tipped up on one side, but he looked more shy than coy.

I couldn't hide my smile. "I have to eat anyway, so it's a sound idea."

We pulled up to my house and the porch light was on, but the rest of the house was dark. I was thankful that I wouldn't have to fight with Maris after coming home from work.

For a few minutes, I sat there having the smallest hope he would lean over and kiss me goodnight. Ky seemed to sense that was what I was waiting for and nipped it in the bud by saying, "I think you should go inside. I'll text you tomorrow before I come over. You can think of where you want to eat before I pick you up."

I nodded, and got out of the car. Knowing Ky was watching, I tried hard not to bounce up the walkway to my door. I was seventeen years old for Heaven's sake. Skipping to the door was something I shouldn't still be doing. I turned once more as I went to step inside.

Ky waved, then pulled away.

Closing the door, I leaned against it and sighed happily.

twelve

. . .

QUESTION: Why was dressing for a date with Ky so much harder than dressing for a date with anyone else?

Answer: Clearly, all boys are not created equal.

I had tried on four different pairs of jeans: skinny ones, capris, straight legged, and a pair I hadn't realized my butt grew out of. I wasn't this indecisive of a person. I put on comfortable clothes and ran with it. The only thing I wasted time with was my cat eye look.

Oh my God! I still had to do makeup!

I was running out of time, and I wanted to impress Ky this afternoon by not looking like I generally did when he saw me at work. I wanted him to see that I put in work for a date with him. I wanted him to know, I didn't take it lightly that he had asked me.

I had decided on the capris, and was pulling out tops that I knew I would only have to change out of once I got to work, when my phone chimed letting me know I had gotten a text.

> Ky: I'm leaving now. I'll be there in 20 minutes.

My mind went into a panic. Twenty minutes?! I grabbed a soft pink V-neck tee that really accentuated the shape of my chest and put my key necklace on before rushing to go do my makeup.

I was debating whether to wear my hair up or down when I heard the doorbell ring. Maris wasn't home, which made me feel a great deal better about the fact that Ky had come to the door. With a quick shake of my head, I decided to leave it down and put a hairband on my wrist so that once I got to work, I could pull it back up.

I nearly fell down the steps, but I made it to the front door with my heart beating so hard, I had to take a breath to compose myself before opening it.

Ky stood on the front porch with his hands in his front pockets which made him appear as if he was incredibly unsure of himself. Something I had never seen him be, ever.

"Hey," he said with a nervous wave.

I couldn't help but grin. So, this was as hard for him as it was for me. Good to know.

"I need to put on my shoes." I pointed to my feet. "Why don't you come in? I'll only be a moment."

A look of panic came across his face. I knew he was worried that Maris was somewhere inside. "She's not here. I don't know where she is, but she's not here," I repeated, so he would chill out some.

He moved slowly, like a feral animal entering unknown territory. My sister really abused the hell out of him. I led him into the living room and sat down to grab my shoes.

Most people had Converse, I had Keds. My favorite pair were my Taylor Swift Black Glitter Dot Keds. My red ones were my lucky ones though. I made a wish and pulled them on and tied them.

Once I was ready, we headed out. I remembered to turn on the porch light, and lock the door, even though my mom hadn't left yet.

Ky kept looking at his feet to the road that led to my driveway nervously. His anxiety was ratcheting up mine two hundred percent. When we got in the car, I decided to lay it all on the line. "I'm really nervous. I took a long time dressing, and I thought I looked really good, but you've looked at everything but me. You are all on edge too, and I can't stand the tension!"

He took a deep breath and exhaled before a self conscious grin spread across his face. "Me too!" he said. "All of it! I spent a half an hour trying to decide which shirt to wear, I thought I was going to throw up from the fuss."

I glanced down at his choice. It was a plain white t-shirt. Seeing where my eyes went, he looked down, and we both started to laugh. It realigned the balance, and we relaxed some.

"Where do you want to go, Jacelyn?" He smiled.

"I was hoping we could go to Marbie's," I suggested, unsure.

Marbie's was another sandwich shop. It was close to work and had the best breaded eggplant sandwich. My mom liked their French dip roast beef ones, and we used to go together with Maris on game nights and get sandwiches before we went to football games. Why we kept going after Maris ripped Ky a new one, I don't know. All she did was rage and eat hot dogs, because she hated Marbie's.

"Marb's sounds good." He turned the engine over, and the car rumbled as he gave it gas and turned around.

I was still nervous, so I licked my lips and started with, "How was school?"

"It was okay. I really only had study hall and Civics." He brushed his hand through his dark hair, and it undid whatever styling he had done to it.

"Two classes on half a day?" I sat forward and turned the radio knob to the college station. A commercial for an upcoming concert came on, and I turned it down. I was getting more nervous again.

"Two study halls." He held up two fingers. "I have mainly AP classes and study halls to do my work in, since I have work after school. Mrs. Kovatch and my dad worked it out the summer before last. The other reason I didn't try to do sports. I can't work as many hours."

I nodded. "Are your college placement classes earning you a lot of units?"

"I'll have my freshman and sophomore Gen Eds finished. How about you? Were you doing dual-enrollment?" He raised a brow.

"I was. I hate talking about it in front of Peter. It's a sore point. But I have twenty four units to transfer because not all my credits from the university out there transfer to units here." I noticed I was talking with my hands, so I sat on them. I sighed frustrated with myself. Awkwardness was my middle name..

We pulled into Marbie's and Ky smiled at me. "Deep breath. We're in this together."

After we ordered and got our food, we got a table outside to eat in the sun. He looked down at his double BLT sandwich. "Does it offend you when I eat meat?"

"No! Does it offend you that I don't?" I countered.

He laughed. "Some vegetarians are offended by meat eaters."

"Yeah, and some meat eaters are offended by vegetarians. I say live your life, and let me live mine. I have been cooking Maris and mom's meals, and it's disgusting, but I've been making them meat meals. I don't want it, but they do. Makes me more and more sure I won't ever be a meat eater."

"Cool, so you'll make me a steak dinner one day?" He grinned.

"Get real, Linley." I made a gagging gesture with my finger in my mouth.

It got quiet while we both munched on our sandwiches and watched people pass by. Ky cleared his throat, "So, I was thinking... about tomorrow..."

I looked at him waiting for him to continue. He looked a little bashful, then he smiled at me and shrugged like he was helpless. "I was wondering how you would feel about us *definitely* calling tomorrow a *date*?"

As I finished my last bite, we got up and started cleaning up our things then walked to the car.

"I thought this was a date," I finally said.

He shook his head in denial. "Can't be. We have work afterward. This is clearly *just* lunch."

"Oh, well I'm disappointed then. I spent all this time and effort getting ready for something that was just a meal and not a date."

"You can consider today a dry run. Tomorrow you'll be an expert." He opened my door and let me in.

"I don't think you can fully understand just how exhausting it was, Ky," I said after he got in on his side. "I'd rather have a more relaxed time."

A wicked grin flashed across his face. "The obvious answer to that, is not to wear any clothing. But since we are going to the movies with Taylor, Sophie and Peter, that would be awkward as hell."

I laughed and nodded. "Going out to the movies naked without Taylor, Sophie and Peter, would also be awkward."

"True." He nodded, licked his lips and turned to me. "We got off topic. I still want to know if you will upgrade our get-together-with-friends to a-date-with-Ky?"

I pretended to give it a moment's consideration before shaking my head. His shoulders fell. "No. I don't think so. It just won't work. We can't have a date, when we have other people with us. It sounds rude. I think you are going to have to give it a shot another time."

I felt pretty brave inviting him to ask me out again.

"I see," came his reply. "You might be right. I'll reserve the offer for tomorrow night. I should wait until the get-together-with-friends is over before I ask you out on Sunday."

"I think you will probably have an excellent chance of getting me to say 'yes,'" I confided.

He grinned. "That sounds promising. If asking you goes well once, I'll probably keep asking."

I couldn't help but chuckle and wink. "Maybe, I'll ask you out before you get a chance to ask me one of these times."

"An independent woman?" He arched an eyebrow. "I don't mind someone who can take control."

"I don't believe in traditional roles," I said. I smiled and teased. "I do believe in the sexist motto that if I pay, you put out though."

I expected him to laugh, but what I got was another bashful look before his eyes darted away, and he started the car.

thirteen

. . .

"SO, today, I am going to get to see how Ky Linley puts the moves on you?" Peter teased while he drove me to the movie theater. Since this wasn't our date, Ky and I had decided to make it as painless as possible, which meant keeping Peter from thinking the worst.

"He has not been making moves on me." I sighed dramatically.

"Hmmm. So have you been making moves on him? Someone has been moving, and I just want to lay blame at the right person's feet." He glanced my way, knowingly.

I rolled my eyes. He wasn't as bad as Maris, but I believed that he would still be a hard sell. I just hoped that he didn't get overly protective today. I was hoping that the five of us could have a nice, relaxing outing to the movies with food after.

I had prayed the night before that neither I, nor Peter, would do anything that could possibly embarrass me.

"What movie are we seeing?" Peter looked at his phone as a text came in, and his jaw dropped. "Quit it!" he whispered.

I didn't know what it said but decided to answer his question. "We haven't decided yet. We are all going to vote on it when we get there. Is there something that you wanted to see? Was the text from Narnia Boy?"

"I don't have a preference and mind your business, Miss Waverly," he sassed.

We were ten minutes from the theater and Peter was dancing in his seat to "Sunshower" by EPEX, when his phone got another text message. He went to reach for it, but I grabbed it and ordered, "Drive! I promise not to look at it, but I won't die at seventeen for you or anyone."

He rolled his eyes and hummed the rest of the song before replying. "I think we should see a comedy. I'm not in the mood for an action movie. Plus, today is going to be dramatic enough without having to see something that will make me cry in front of everyone."

Peter was a big crier. When we watched the *Notebook,* he cried for fifteen minutes at the end. And whenever we watch *Hunger Games,* he bawled through the selection when Prim got picked and Katniss volunteered. He was so loud that my mom came down one night to see if he was okay. Don't get him started on *The Farewell*, he will never recover from that movie because he identified with the Asians in it.

"Do you know Sophie or Taylor?" I wondered since Peter was a gossip, and Ky admitted that Sophie and Peter's crush are besties.

"Sophie is really sweet. I don't know anything about Taylor, other than he geeks out on his Nintendo Switch or PSP, or whatever it is he's into whenever he has freetime. Sophie says he's into gaming, so I might have strung all those words together from things I've heard on TV about video games.

"The group eats lunch together–which you've already been told a million times. They are pretty tight. The hot guy table and cheerleaders have been ignored by him to the point where they barely try anymore."

"Yet, you still think he's a baddie?" I leveled him with my best you're-full-of-shit look.

Peter turned into the movie theater entrance and waved away my comment. "I haven't seen him digging in the rich soil, Jacelyn. But that doesn't mean he isn't dirty."

I was so frustrated. Everything I heard from him and Mare said he was different, but they didn't believe their own words.

When we grouped up with everyone, it was an awkward meeting and everyone stood around for a few moments. Ky's sister and brother were incredibly good look- ing, clearly favoring Ky in that aspect. Finally, Sophie stepped forward and hugged me. "It's so nice to meet you. I'm Sophie."

"Jacelyn," I introduced myself, needlessly.

She looked at Peter and spilled the tea. "Gaven couldn't come."

"Gaven?" I asked, eyebrows raised. "Would this be Narnia Boy?"

"Narnia Boy?" Sophie asked.

"The boy that lives in his closet," I replied.

She bit her lip and laughed quietly, her shoulders shak- ing. "That sounds suspiciously like my best friend. You call him Narnia Boy?"

I nodded. "I wasn't allowed to know his name because Peter was protecting his identity like it was an endangered species. You just let the cat out of the bag."

Her jaw dropped. "Oh shizwhit."

Peter grabbed her and wrapped her in a hug and whispered something in her ear, and they both nearly fell down laughing.

I looked over at Taylor who was looking at his phone. "So what are you doing?"

"Playing Pokémon Go. There is a level five raid here, and there are three people in it. I'm inviting friends to join me." He came over to me to show his screen, and I saw a list of names with green dots next to them. "I just select the ones that are online and hope for the best."

Ky grabbed my hand and pulled me to him. "He won't stop if you stand there. He will start telling you about stats, fighting abilities, hundos, shundos, and legendaries. Just to start. What do you want to watch?"

"I want to see the new exorcism movie!" Taylor grinned.

"NO!" The four of us chorused back.

"The new superhero movie looks really good," Sophie said. "Those are always funny."

"Meh," Peter responded with an unimpressed look. "What about the Margot Robbie one?"

I looked over the options. "What about the Tom Hardy one? He's super hot!"

Ky snorted. "Can't argue when the movie looks dope."

"I'll go see the Superhero," Taylor said, creating a tie.

"Wow, this is some super suckage. Okay, I'll buy dinner for anyone who will come see the Margot Robbie movie!" Peter held up his hand looking for volunteers and Sophie, Taylor and Ky all raised their hands.

"Peter, you're so dumb, you didn't ask where we're going first!" I looked at everyone. "Where do you eat Saturday dinner?"

Taylor rubbed his hands together. "Traditionally, it's Fresno's."

Peter's shoulders slumped, and I raised my hand. "I'm

in too. Let's go see the Margot Robbie movie!" I crowed, pumping my fists in the air.

Despite it not being a date, Ky bought my ticket and walked into the theater holding my hand. When we got to the counter, he whispered in my ear, "Could you go with Sophie and Taylor to get seats? I'm going to hang out with Peter and grab some refreshments."

Peter turned around as I looked at him. "What?"

"Ky is going to stay with you while I go get our seats, I guess?" I said, sounding like an idiot.

My best friend laughed. "Don't be sad, it just took holding your sweaty palm for him to realize he liked boys."

I shook my head and pushed him as I walked by meeting Sophie and Taylor who were still apparently playing Pokémon Go.

We chose the seats in the back of the theater. To be honest, I didn't care where we sat, as long as we were comfortable. When the Linleys arranged themselves, Taylor took the seat next to me and Sophie sat next to him. She smiled at me. "Peter can sit with me."

I nodded at her then got straight up nervous. My hands got sweaty. My feet were tingly. Taylor leaned over and whispered, "Breathe, Jacelyn."

I took a deep, shaky breath and laughed. "I'm such a nerd."

"No, I'm a nerd." He held up his game. "I play, so I don't have to socialize."

"You're socializing right now," I replied.

He smirked and it was so much like Ky's, that I felt myself grin at the familiarity. "Ever play?"

"No. Tell me about it," I said as the ads came on.

Taylor grinned and showed me his Trainer, whose name was 'TayinNSlayin.' "This is my trainer code and when you start playing, you and I will exchange codes and be friends."

"4396 6161 7952 is you?" I asked.

"Yep, that's my trainer code, and I will be friends with anyone who adds me." He grinned.

"And I'm supposed to start playing so we can be friends?" I clarified.

"Don't make me keep repeating myself. You don't look dumb," Taylor said then blushed.

"Woah!" I sat back in my seat and chuckled.

Some film facts started to come up on the screen, and Sophie and I started a trivia challenge while we waited. I had no idea what was taking Ky and Peter so long. Finally, the two appeared with their arms full of goods that nearly overflowed.

"I got you a lemonade, no ice," Ky said, handing me my drink. I didn't realize he was paying enough attention at work to realize I took it that way.

Peter sat down on Sophie's other side and handed the bag of popcorn to me to share. "This is really inconvenient," he commented.

"I'll switch." Taylor got up so he and Peter could swap seats.

Once next to me, Peter whispered in my ear, "No groping or making out in the movie, I have a sensitive gag reflex."

I turned to him and poked him hard in the side, hoping Ky and his siblings hadn't heard his comment.

Throughout the movie, I was aware of Ky holding my hands because Peter elbowed me and hummed in my ear whenever he noticed. It was like having a disapproving grandmother with us.

After the movie, we decided to go somewhere cheaper

than Fresno's since Peter insisted on paying, and we ended up at Perkins. I got in Peter's car and immediately started grilling him. "What happened when you two went to get snacks, What did you talk about?"

"Do you mean... 'Peter, did he talk about me?' or 'Tell me everything that came out of his mouth, word for word, breath by breath, and please analyze every twitch of his nose?'" He smirked.

"Don't be ridiculous." I rolled my eyes. "And don't be a jerk. What did you talk about?"

Peter's lips flattened. "Well he doesn't like Sno-Caps, and he was pretty disappointed that they didn't have pretzel M&M's." I whined while Peter merged into the turning lane.

"Is that all?" I didn't know if I was happy or disappointed that they hadn't magically mended fences. Was it too much to ask them to have left the refreshment counter at a ceasefire?

"He may have also taken a moment to tell me that he knew that he had really acted like a complete asshole in the past. He asked me if there was any way for him to make it up to you or to me and Mare so we would think better of him. He also made a promise to me he would not hurt you like that again." He pursed his lips and sighed.

I couldn't help the smile that stretched across my face. "See, I told you that he was different."

"Jace, I'm not sure what to believe. I don't mean to hold a grudge—it might be Connie Kim *actually* living in my head, or just listening to Mare for the last few years bashing your boyfriend over and over again. He made it sound like he had good intentions, but I'm not ready to forget what he did to my best friend. I know you want me to tell you that I approve, and I'm behind you two dating or whatever, but I can't. I will do you a favor and reserve my disapproval while you take it very slow with him. I mean very, very slow.

"I'm not gonna run interference for you and Maris though. Your sister is a whole other thing, altogether. What I will do is, I'll make an effort to check him out at school and not freeze him out. I'm not making a promise to become his best friend, but I'll talk to him and be civil."

I laughed out loud happily and squealed. As soon as he parked, I reached over and hugged him. What he was saying was, he didn't trust Ky, but he trusted me. That was all I wanted. "Thank you. I won't disappoint you."

"I know you won't." He hugged me back. "Don't get hurt, Jacelyn. I'll have to gay boy hurt him, and that is melodramatic shit."

I left the car with a smile too large for my face and grabbed Ky's hand when I saw him and squeezed it twice. Sophie saw it, smiled, and bit her lip, like she had somehow had a hand in it. If she did, I was thankful.

The Perkins' green and white awnings flapped in the breeze, and I wrapped my arms around myself. It was still a little cool at night. The bright lights of the parking lot threw harsh shadows on our faces, and I couldn't help but grin happily that we were all together. When we got to the door, Taylor gave his brother a knowing look. There was some sort of competition brewing there.

We slid into a U-shaped green and black booth and got our menus and the waitress took our drink orders. Peter leaned over to Taylor and asked, "I know nothing about video games, what kind do you like?"

"Mainly I play MMO, games with lore and stories. I like fantasy based games. I'm not too into first person shooter games or strategy games. I do play them sometimes though with friends and Ky." He played with the condensation on his Dr. Pepper, and nodded his head like he agreed with himself.

"Pretend I followed that." Peter smiled. "What are some of your favorite games?"

"I like *WoW*, *World Of Warcraft*. Ky and I play together, and it's extra. There are always new things to do and because it's an MMO and other people are playing, you never really have to worry about not having someone to play with." He smiled at his brother.

I vaguely knew the game from people I hung out with in SoCal. "Isn't that the game where you get to make your character and it can be like a sorcerer or a magician or barbarian?"

"I guess, sort of. There are toons, right?" Taylor became animated at this point and moved his glass and started talking with his hands. "Mages, Warlocks, Death Knights... Warriors, just to name a few. I have five toons at level 70, two at level 65, and a Monk I just started." I was bowled over by how much he looked like Ky when he spoke about his family. Not to mention the same dark hair and gray eyes. He was going to be a heartbreaker when he got older.

I turned to Ky to include him in the conversation. "What do you play?"

He got a lopsided smile on his face. "I have a few toons. Only two are level 70, a Hunter and a Priest. I started a Monk with Taylor, and we've been leveling them together. Taylor has some good names for his toons."

Peter leaned in. "What names are they?"

He smiled bigger than I thought was imaginable "My main toon is Elan, he's a Mage, and I've been playing him for about two years. Ky's got the coolest toon name though. His Priest's name is Disperse. She's named after a special spell that they have to gain mana."

I nodded at him like I was getting it all, but they'd lost me when they had started talking to me about the different kinds of classes and specs. I was sure that it was simple stuff for someone who played the game, but it was nonsense to someone who didn't.

"Do you play video games?" Taylor asked me.

"I watched friends play *Among Us*. But I've never played," I admitted.

Taylor nodded at my comment and smiled.

"Maybe I can come watch you play sometime," I offered.

"Yeah, you could come over, and we could get you set up with a toon on Soph's computer, and the three of us can play!" he said excitedly.

Our waitress was a woman who looked tired, and we learned she was at the end of her shift. We got our food, and Ky waved her near with two fingers. "If we gave you your tip now would you be able to transfer the check and leave?"

Her shoulders relaxed as she sighed in relief. "Are you tipping in cash?"

I smiled. "We can."

"You'd do that?" She looked like she was going to cry. I have to go get my son from the babysitter, she can't watch him any later tonight. She has class in–" She looks at her watch. "Less than an hour."

Peter, Sophie, Ky and I all got out cash which was much more than a normal tip and handed it to her, and her jaw dropped. "You guys!" She covered her mouth. "Thank you."

Peter ate quietly and watched Sophie, Ky and I talk, taking it all in. As soon as we were done though, he didn't linger. He looked at his phone and nodded his chin to the door. "We should head out."

Sophie stood and hugged him. "Give me your phone."

He handed it over, and she plugged in her number and smiled. "Text me tomorrow, and we can figure out when we can go see another movie. Also, I'm always down to gossip about Gav!"

Peter blushed, and I laughed.

When we were pulling out of the parking lot, I noticed he seemed troubled. "What's up? Did you have a bad time at Perkins?"

"No!" He sighed. "It was good. Sophie is cool to hang out with, and whatever Taylor was saying about video games was enlightening–sort of. I think that when you defect to the land of girl-with-boyfriend, I'll make her my fag hag and adopt him."

"So you're replacing me? That was quick." I smiled. "What's wrong?"

He ignored my last question and teased, reaching over and patting my knee. "There comes a time in every relationship where the vital question arises, 'How do I best fulfill my own needs?' and we've reached it."

I laughed. I knew he was giving me a hard time. Peter and I would end up in the same old person's home sharing Motrin and Blue-Emu. "So you are going to see a chick-flick with Sophie sometime?" I kept poking, looking to see if I could find what troubled him and had shut him down at dinner.

"Well, I would invite you, but you are always at work. Plus, I know how you get after a chick-flick. You are aware that happy endings exist, right?" He gave me a sad smile.

After my dad left my mom, chick-flicks took a brutal setback from me. I felt that the fireworks and touching moments at the end of a romance movie was a sham. I believed that in real life, emotions were more subtle and nothing could ever be that perfect, and if it felt that way–it probably wouldn't survive.

Peter, on the other hand, had admitted to dreaming of being the recipient of one of those powerful knee weakening kisses just before the ending credits.

"How 'bout you, Jacelyn? Did you have a good time? Boy-toy surprised me at the restaurant by being so nice to the waitress." He sounded like he didn't like being surprised by that.

We were almost to my house as I responded. "I had a really good time. I think I proved to you that Ky and I could control our overwhelming passion, and I could sit next to him without humping his leg, in either the movie or restaurant. I told you you had nothing to fear about my behavior in public. I'm even housetrained and no longer potty on the floor."

Peter tsked me. "I could see it in your eyes. You were terribly close. I can barely let you near such a good looking guy without you fluttering your eyelashes and showing your gams. You're heading for deep waters with that one, and you're just lucky I'm on lifeguard duty."

"Gams? Did you get that one from Humphrey Bogart?" I grinned.

"I did!" He laughed.

"Are you coming in while I make dinner for Mare?" I asked, as we pulled into my driveway and saw Alex's car at the house.

"What are you making?" Peter asked

I shrugged. "Something quick, I guess. Angel hair Bolognese?"

He made a face. "Isn't that a fancy way to say little noodles in meat sauce?"

I laughed. "Are you asking all these questions because you are hungry again? You didn't eat a lot at the restaurant."

"Maybe for a bit." He shrugged. "I haven't seen much of Mare this week. If she and Alex aren't getting it on, maybe I can say 'hey' and hang out."

"Why do you keep deflecting?" I asked as we got out of the car. When he didn't reply, I grunted out his name, "Peter Kim!"

"It's nothing. I just have things on my mind. I can think about things and not tell you about them," he said with bite and attitude, opening my front door.

We separated at the door awkwardly.

While I cooked, Peter, Maris and Alex sat in the living room talking. When I entered the living room for a little while, my sister looked up at me and quickly looked away. I could assume from that, Peter had been talking about today in anticipation of our movie hang out.

I lifted a hand toward the TV. "Do you guys want to put on a movie?"

Maris gave an unenthused shrug and Alex said nothing, just flattened his lips. Peter reached for the Amazon Fire remote, "I'm picking out the movie. Last time, Alex picked out Transformers and Megan Fox is no one I find attractive."

"Tom Hardy!" I tried again for the second time today.

Peter glanced at me and rolled his eyes. "I was thinking of Justin Timberlake. I love *Friends With Benefits*."

"Why do we always have to watch older movies?" Mare asked.

Alex and Peter shrugged. "Newer ones suck," Alex explained.

Mare grabbed the remote and scrolled to find the Netflix app and clicked on Bridgerton. Alex and I groaned.

Peter squealed and flopped down on the couch with her and started talking about the plot.

I went back in the kitchen to check the sauce, and Alex followed me.

"I know you aren't trying to piss Mare off, but she's never going to let this go," he said.

"I'm not trying to make it difficult. Ky's–you know what, I'm not going to defend him to you. Just tell me why you don't talk to him anymore." I stirred the sauce then put the flame down so it simmered.

"When he pulled away, I found out later why, with his mom being sick and everything. I tried to be there for him, but he kept blowing me off. Then I got with your sister. She has no affection for him, and it was better to not try to mix them." He shrugged. "I guess, I'm the asshole in the equation, but I don't want Mare hurt. She's been hurt enough."

I nodded. "That's good of you, I'm glad you care about her so much. But my life can't revolve around her feelings or anyone else's. Mare doesn't even care about my feelings, and I'm tired of having to explain myself. I shouldn't have to."

He sighed, and as he turned to walk out of the kitchen, my phone chimed signaling a text, and he grabbed it off the table to walk over and hand it to me.

I glance down at the message and tilt my head in confusion.

+1 (570) 555-0885: When do you think you can come over?

Me: Who is this?

+1 (570) 555-0885: It's Taylor. You want to come over and play some video games?

. . .

I couldn't help but smile. It was fairly obvious how Taylor got my number. I was wondering how much of this was Taylor wanting me to come over and how much was Ky being sly.

Me: I don't work on Tuesday night. I could come over then. Do I buy the game or game system and study how to play before then?

+1 (570) 555-0885: I don't think you need to go that far. Ky and I will teach you how to play. Although, you should prepare to low-key suck when you start.

Me: Oh, I don't have to prepare, it's a given.

+1 (570) 555-0885: Cool. See you Tuesday. Kk?

Me: What's Kk?

+1 (570) 555-0885: *laughing emoji* It's how I say okay?

Me: Are you telling me or asking me?

+1 (570) 555-0885: Talk to you Tuesday, Jacelyn!

Me: Tell your brother next time he wants a date, to do his own dirty work.

Nothing came after that, so I wasn't sure what to make of it. I added his number to my contacts under his Pokémon Go name: TayinNSlayin. I looked up to find Mare studying me, her expression was mulish. "It wasn't even him!" I said defensively.

"And I don't believe you!" She turned and walked out of the room. Next I heard, "Alex, get me the hell out of here!"

fourteen

. . .

"JACELYN! There is a creep at the door saying he is giving you a ride to work!" Maris' voice carried upstairs. I felt sorry for Ky for running into her but was pretty proud of the fact that he came to my door. I gave myself one more lookover and headed out the bedroom door and down the stairs. When I got to the foyer and didn't see him, I went into the living room where Maris was. "Where is he?"

"Out on the porch, where I'd keep any dog. I'm never allowing that bastard in *this* house," she seethed.

I rolled my eyes and opened the door to find him standing on the top step looking out at the yard. I know I'm a little pervy, but I totally checked out his butt. I blamed his jeans, they drew my attention to his backside.

"We should get going," I said. He turned and gave me a smile. I tilted my head, and my brows furrowed. "Sorry about Mare."

"Yeah, well I expected nothing less. Actually, she super-seded expectations. She did talk to me when she opened the door." He smiled more.

I widened my eyes and waited for him to share what my sister had to say to him.

He laughed and looked away. "She asked me what the hell I wanted and if I was looking to die today."

I made a pained expression, then laughed at the absurdity. "Well, the good thing about Mare is that you never have to worry about where you stand with her. She is always transparent."

He nodded, chuckled and kicked his foot out. "She makes no secret of her feelings, I agree. I just wish..." He took a deep breath and shook his head. I grabbed his hand and pulled him to his car and looked back to see the curtain twitch. I knew my sister was watching, but I didn't care anymore. Like she didn't have a lot of time with Alex. I might not have a lot of time with Ky. I didn't even know what was really happening with my relationship with him, but I wasn't going to let her decide what I would do with him.

Work was pretty uneventful. Melissa was off for a wedding, and the morning shift worker, Leslie, was covering. He was really laid back. Nothing seemed to concern him, and Mel's orderly refrigerator and bins were obliterated. I spent the night trying to reorganize and keep up with everything.

It was also busy as all get-out. Deliveries were one after another, and I saw little of Ky until Ricky came back and told Leslie to take his lunch. All the tension had left our interactions and was replaced with playful flirtation.

"So if I'm coming over on Tuesday, what time are you picking me up?" I grinned at him.

Ky looked at me a little surprised. "You're coming over on Tuesday?"

131

I gave him a perplexed look. "Taylor texted me last night and asked me. I thought you had him invite me."

He tried to hide the smile that was blooming on his face. "My brother texted you, huh?"

Now I felt uncomfortable. What if Ky didn't want me to come over. "Yeah, I didn't realize you didn't know. I don't have to come over. It must have sounded a little rude the way I asked you to pick me up."

He shook his head. "No, no. That's fine. I would really like to have you come over. I'm just surprised is all. Blown away actually, with how Taylor is behaving with you. It's pretty unheard of for him to talk to girls. He's generally freaked out by them. I'm thinking he has a crush on you. It must be something in the Linley family genetics. If that's the case then maybe you shouldn't meet my dad."

I laughed knowing full well Ky was safe there. From everything I heard, his dad adored his wife. "So, am I coming over then?"

Ky couldn't hide his smile this time. "I don't know, are you? When's your car getting here?"

"My dad said it's delayed. Are you complaining about having to drive me?" I grinned. My face was starting to hurt from all the smiling. I hated how excited I was at the idea. I had to remind myself that Taylor invited me and not Ky.

"I don't mind driving you around. It's like a captive audience. But you didn't answer my other question." He turned and looked at one of the tickets.

"I'd like to come over. You have school so maybe you can pick me up on your way home? Three-thirty?" I suggested.

"Is this a date?" He was straight up grinning then. His right eyebrow popped up in speculation.

"Nope, this is a playdate between me and Taylor. He

invited me. But I expect you to supply the grape juice boxes and the fruit roll-ups," I teased.

He nodded. "Of course. What flavors?"

"I like strawberry, but electric blue raspberry is acceptable." I went to the fridge and started sorting the mess. We couldn't just flirt the entire time he was back here, or Ricky would fire us!

"I'm on it, like white on rice!" I laughed at his excitement. "But I think it's crap that my brother has a date with you before I do."

"You snooze, you lose!" I shook a finger at him.

He snorted and started putting together a parm dish.

Leslie came back and insisted that I learn how to make pizzas. We were behind on pies, and he thought I would quicken the orders–I didn't. I thought I made it worse.

It was later than normal leaving work because clean-up ran over, but as I got into Ky's car that night, I was sad because I wasn't ready for the night to end. He surprised me though, he turned my way and said, "Where are we going tonight?"

I bit my lip. "Don't you have school tomorrow?"

"I do, but I can sleep in study hall. It's the last few weeks. We're doing a review, and I'm extra smart. I'll be good. I'm thinking we go to Maystown, go to the grocery store and stock up on snacks for when my brother's new girlfriend comes over on Tuesday night," he teased with a smirk.

I let the comment go, and nodded. "Let's go!" All night grocery stores had never held much appeal, but when we pulled into Wegman's, there were more cars than I had thought there would be.

"Do we need a cart?" I asked as we headed inside.

He shook his head and grabbed a handbasket.

I looked around as we stood in the bakery. "Where to first? I assume we aren't here for a loaf of rye."

"Always start in the candy aisle," he said, like it was the quintessential beginning to any grocery store visit and took off.

I ran to catch up to him. "I have to admit, I don't know the precise rules and etiquette for a midnight trip to the grocery store. Do I need to write this down?"

He nodded. "Oh, there will be a written and oral exam at the end of this. I had to take it a few times before I passed. All I can tell you is that there is no curve."

I loved that he could be goofy. I was never one for heavy and serious. The easy way he and I had banter and fun made me feel better about trusting him. It wasn't just his charm though. He felt good in my heart.

"Now, are you writing this down?" He looked at me. "You have to know first, one thing about yourself... are you a chocolate or a gummy person?

I gave it some thought and looked at each sort of candy on the shelf. "I really think I'm a chocolate person."

"Are you a Hershey, Nestlé, Godiva, Cadbury, or Ghirardelli kind of girl?" He pointed at each one.

I looked at him instead of the chocolate. "Can't I be all of them?" I turned and looked at them like they were long lost lovers. "Do I have to have a favorite?"

He shook his head. "No. You can be as indiscriminate as you'd like." He then moved to the other side of me. "Next question. Milk chocolate, dark chocolate or white chocolate? Almonds, peanuts, or pretzels? Raspberry, cherry or orange? You have an array here to start your selection."

"No wonder why there is a written exam on selecting candy. You really have to think this out." I looked at the shelves. "I like Godiva Dark Chocolate with Raspberries,

Ghirardelli Dark Chocolate with Mint, Reese's Peanut Butter Cups and Butterfingers." I watched him pick up one of each and add them to the basket. When I noticed he didn't add anything for himself, I pointed into it and narrowed my eyes. "What about you? Chocolate or gummy?"

"Oh, you've got the hang of this already. I'm a Swedish Fish kinda guy."

"There are different flavors like original, grape, multi-colored and Aqua." I arched an eyebrow waiting for him to share his preference.

He shrugged. "I'm a traditionalist." He reached out and grabbed a three pound bag of red Swedish fish and put it in our basket.

I nodded slowly then bursted out in a fit of laughter.I grabbed a bag of party-sized Peanut M&M's and started walking to our next destination. "Where to next?"

He pointed in the direction of the back of the store. "Next, we get drinks. Personally, I recommend water. Candy goes down best with water."

I nodded. "You seem to have a system. I'm going to go with your recommendation since you appear to be the expert."

When we got to the water, he started the spiel, "Aqua-fina, Arrowhead, Evia–"

I cut him off. "I think we have to go with Fiji. I know my water, and I'm telling you it's the only one worthy of the name water."

He nodded seriously like I had just given the most intel-ligent suggestion there was. "Now, ice cream." He grabbed my hand and started pulling me in the direction of the frozen treats section.

"Does ice cream go with candy?' I asked, skeptically.

He threw a look of disbelief over his shoulder. "Are you telling me that you think birthday parties everywhere are doing it wrong?"

I chuckle. "I think you are thinking of cake and ice cream."

"Fine, fancy pants, we'll go back to the bakery and get cake next. Right now, what flavors are we getting?" He pointed at the single serving cups. "Do I need to start listing your selections?"

"No, I think I got this," I said, grabbing a Häagan-Dazs Dulce de Leche cup. He smiled and grabbed a Ben & Jerry's Chunky Monkey. They were then added to our basket. My hand was once again in Ky's as he pulled me along to the bakery where they had single slices of different cakes.

"I have to admit, I'm new to the cake portion of the midnight trip to the grocery store. What flavor do you recommend?" Ky tilted his head and surveyed the options.

I peered over the selection and grabbed a red velvet cake slice and a lemon cake and put them in our now overflowing basket of treasures.

He pointed to the small container of forks near the display. "We are going to need these too." I grabbed them and slipped them into my purse.

I was shocked when our shopping spree came to sixty dollars. That was a lot of money to spend to maximize our dental bills. When I tried to split it with him, he pushed my hand back and said, "I'm buying this time. You get the next trip." Which made me smile and blush. God, I hoped this became a regular thing.

When we got back in the car, we opened the bag between us and started to divvy up our items. "We need to eat the ice cream first," he advised.

I peeled the plastic cover from mine and put it in the

bag, which I designated would be for our garbage. "It's handy that they have the little spoons in the cups!" I clicked it out and held out the little ice cream shovel. "Can I have a bite of yours?" I asked.

He held out his spoon and without asking, I did the same.

"I have to say I like yours better than mine." He smacked his lips. "A point for Häagan-Dazs. I'll have to get one of theirs next time."

I nodded. "It's creamier."

"Well, mine is called *Chunky* Monkey." He held up his and pointed at the name.

"Let's hope it's not *too* literal and made of real monkeys," I joked.

It was nearly one-thirty when I noticed the time, and we were only three quarters through our sugar fest and most of the chocolate hadn't been touched yet. I found spending time with Ky always passed faster than I wanted it to.

I pointed at his three pound bag of fish that he had put a dent into, and he brought it closer to his body as if he were protecting it from me. "I think you should give me a few fish."

"What are you going to give me for them?" he asked with narrowed eyes.

I looked at his mouth and then his eyes. "I'll give you a kiss."

He shook his head. "No. No, that comes at the end of a date. We haven't had an actual date yet. You've eaten a lot of what I'd be down to try, but you don't have much to barter with. I don't like peanut butter."

"What are you? A monster? Who doesn't like peanut butter, it's an American staple. There is Skippy, Jif, Peter Pan and Smuckers..." I listed them, and he laughed.

"Peanut butter is vile. What do you have left? You ate your cake didn't you?" He peered into my lap.

"I have a Butterfinger." I held it up.

He took a minute to consider it then nodded. I held out my candy bar for him to take a bite, and at the last moment, he looked up at me and froze. There was something in his eyes. It felt like he wanted something far more than just my candy bar. Maybe that kiss I ached for wasn't mine to ache for alone.

But then the moment passed, and he smiled and took a bite.

"Disgusting. It's peanut butter." He makes a face with his tongue stuck out.

"We need to stop having gatherings and just have a date already," I said, my voice held a breathless quality that was embarrassing in its misery.

He smiled crookedly. "It's bound to happen someday."

fifteen

. . .

MARIS SAT across from me at the breakfast table. She was angry because dad called this morning at six a.m. to be sure to talk to me and attempted to talk to her before school. My car was still unfortunately held hostage. Currently, Maris was ignoring me by watching TikTok videos.

"You know, Mare... it doesn't matter how long you punish me, it won't change things or make me do things I don't want to do."

"Who says that I'm punishing you?" she snarled. I could hear the defensive tone in her voice that told us both, she was definitely doing just that.

"I don't want to go out with Trick–like ever again," I bit out. "I wish you could respect that without this ridiculous tantrum. It's hard to believe right now that you are the older sister. How would you feel if I wanted to set you up with someone I knew from San Diego, while you were here all day pining away for Alex."

"That's different, Jacelyn. Number one, I love Alex. We are dating exclusively, and he is my boyfriend. You don't have a boyfriend, and the guy you like is sus, period. I worry for you. For someone so smart, you act like you are shitidiot. Number two, I can't sit by and watch dad 2.0 take out another member of this family. I won't do it. You're wrong if you think you won't be just like mom paying with emotional cash for being with an asshole," she barked out at me, red faced and watery eyed.

"And, so that I won't pay later, you're going to make me pay for it now. What the hell is that?" I gave her a look, disappointed with how unfair she was being.

She shrugged in response and gave all her attention to her phone.

"So, that's it? You're going to be angry at me forever?" I huffed.

Maris looked at me, annoyed. "No! I'm going to stay mad at you until you stop seeing Ky Linley and talking to dad. I'm going to tell you 'I told you so,' when Ky does you dirty and then I'm going to laugh when you tell me to hook you up with Trick!" Her voice rose with the last words as she pointed an accusing finger at me.

I tried to swallow my disbelief at her statements and laid my hands flat on the table, so I didn't start returning her pointing and aggressive hand movements. I took a deep breath and tried to maturely handle all her defined points. "I can't believe you want to give me an ultimatum on dad. No matter what he's done, he's our blood. He's an asshole, you're right, and he made a world's worth of mistakes, but we don't turn our back on family. EVER!

"It's not surprising that your next ultimatum is on Ky. It's not a reality or possibility for you to live both of our lives, Maris. You get one, not two. Worry about your own. It goes without saying that your life... it's not perfect." I shook my head. "It's the fact that you are waiting to say, I told you so, and laugh in my face that makes me wonder if you love me at all or if I'm merely another doll in your dollhouse. No wonder you couldn't get rid of your collection upstairs. You like to pretend you have control over other people's actions."

She slumped in her chair shaking her head. As if she didn't listen to a word I said, she went on to harp on a topic I was done with. "Trick is a good person, I've known him for a while. He doesn't treat girls badly."

"Mare, you need a hearing exam. He likes Rosa Easton, and I don't care if he makes every girl he meets a princess. The point isn't that he does or doesn't treat anyone well. It's that I genuinely don't like him romantically, and I don't want to date him!" I squeezed my eyes shut in frustration and tried very hard to keep it together. She was testing my last nerve.

"Ky's not the right guy for you. He's sketchy, he always has been and always will be." Tears spilled out from her eyes and down her cheeks.

I shook my head. I could hear my voice rising. "When was the last time you spent any time with him? When did you last talk to him like he was a person? Or even treat him like he was a person? People make mistakes. It's a part of life. We're all imperfect regardless of how you see yourself."

I knew once anyone started yelling, people stopped communicating. I was close to yelling. There had been so much yelling in this house the last few months before my mom found out about my dad, and they got a divorce. I hated that the yelling was happening again.

My sister slammed her hand down on the table. "Why? Why should I do that? I don't care what Ky would ever have to say. I'm a good person, I don't hang out with people like him. So are you. It doesn't matter all the good things he does now. All the bad things stack up against him, and they don't go away. There are no second chances."

I felt everything in me deflate. "I never saw you as a bigot before, but you are acting like one now. You're my sister, and I love you more than words could ever say, but you make me sick with the way you think of people these days. You're narrow-minded and hateful as shit. I was hoping we could find a way to work through this. A 'live and let live' solution that would help us both find some happiness, but I just realized you aren't a happy person, and you want everyone around you to be just as miserable. You're stubborn, a little dumb and can't consider anything other than what you've convinced yourself is true or real. I don't know how you can have a relationship with Alex because you are so committed to your delusions. I hope he never does anything that displeases you, because the poor guy won't get... What was that? No second chances." I was all out yelling now and from the steps of my mother coming down the hall, my screeching carried through the house.

"What is wrong with you two? Why are you having a shouting match at seven a.m.? I didn't get home until after three. I *want* to sleep. No–I *need* it!" She stood in front of us, rubbing her eyes, in a tee that said, 'ASSES are something you RIDE... PLEASE DO NOT PINCH,'

I instantly felt guilty. "Sorry, mom. Maris and I are having a disagreement."

"Is this something that I need to solve for you two, or can you both act like adults and solve it for yourselves? You aren't little girls anymore, I can't just separate seven year olds who can't agree on which dolly they play with. Can you two figure this out without bringing the roof down?!" she said forcefully, sounding exhausted.

From outside, a car horn sounded and Maris stood. "According to Jace, I'm the one who acts like she's seven, and Jace is my dolly. Apparently, I'm an immature bigot who can't let things go. The truth is, that she has shit taste in little boys who will never act like men. I'm done with this, I'm out of here."

As she left the house, the front door slammed and rattled the framed painting mom had on the wall of a bottle of wine with grapes in front of it in the foyer.

My mom sighed. "Alright, Jacie, I'm awake now, you might as well lay it on me," my mother said, moving into the kitchen. She went to the cupboard and pulled down her instant coffee and made herself a cup, before shuffling to the table.

I went to the counter and picked up two of the pancakes I had made and brought them to her. Maris hadn't touched hers. I sat down and leaned my head on my hand. "Mare's completely unhinged because I've started seeing Ky outside of work. She has a colossal-sized grudge against him, and she won't give either him or me a break. This morning, she gave me an ultimatum on dad and him. I choose Trick and her or them. And when Ky leaves me, which she is positive he will do in an embarrassing fashion, she will laugh and say 'I told you so.'"

My mom sipped her coffee and shook her head. "Maris is still very angry at your father for what happened. I have her seeing the counselor at school and a therapist. She likes to think she has control over things. Unplanned events make her anxious. She is very imma-ture for her age. Or maybe she is just compared to you. It doesn't help though that everything with her is black and white, all one or the other. There is no abstract in her world yet, and it's going to hurt her when she learns that lesson."

My mom wasn't telling me anything I hadn't just screamed at my sister.

I inhaled and exhaled softly. "Should I not see the guy I like just to keep the peace?"

She smiled. "I don't want you to grow up a people pleaser, or an apologist. You only have one life to live. If you spend it pleasing everyone, you will resent everyone and yourself in the end. If you feel like you have to apologize all the time for the choices you make, you will always question yourself.

"If you like Ky, then you should date him. You're only seventeen and hopefully you have a good seventy or eighty years ahead of you to sort out all the heavy stuff. Even if Maris never accepts him, your happiness is what's important.

"We have to be realistic with Maris though. She has Alex, and if you didn't like him, she wouldn't give him up for you or anyone. Bring over Ky. I'd like to meet him. I promise you that I won't judge him on anything other than the impression he makes when I see him interact with you now. I will also let Mare know she isn't welcome to be part of that visit."

I smiled. My mom was pretty awesome. A lot of mothers would fret over being told a guy was no good, but my mom liked to think for herself. I was pretty secure in the fact Ky would leave her with a good opinion of him.

She stood and headed to the sink with her cup. "If this is sorted. I'd like to go lay down. Having that coffee was probably not a good idea. Thankfully, I'm not working tonight."

"Mom?" I walked over and hugged her tightly.

"Awww." She squeezed me back. "I love you, Jacelyn."

"When should I have Ky over?"

She leaned back and smiled. "I don't work Friday this week."

"We work Friday night, but he has half a day. Maybe he can come during the day?" I asked with hope in every word.

My mom nodded. "Fine. You're cooking, and I'll handle getting rid of your sister."

"If I cook more often, can we get rid of her permanently?" I joked.

"Jacelyn!" my mother's voice raised in warning as she headed to her room.

sixteen

. . .

> ThatPizzaKy: I'm going to leave in 10 minutes. Will that give you enough time to get ready?

KY HAD MESSAGED me earlier that Sophie wasn't feeling well and didn't drive to school today, and he had to drive her home before coming to get me. He apologized profusely at the change of plans, even though it was no big deal.

> Me: I will be ready in about 5 minutes. You really should hurry before I change my mind, put on pajamas and start watching the cooking channel.

> ThatPizzaKy: I will leave in 2 then and break the land speed record. Is it okay if I have my head through the arm hole of my shirt and my pants on inside out when I get there? You aren't giving me a lot of time to dress to impress.

> Me: LOL I guess that I can give you a few minutes to put on clothes.

> Me: Wait a second! Does this mean you are texting me in the nude?!!

It took a few minutes for his reply to come.

> ThatPizzaKy: Not anymore *tongue sticking out emoji* I'm leaving now!

I got my makeup on. I had a YouTube tutorial for summer eyes playing, and I had gotten the eyeshadow that it recommended. They looked more natural than summery but brighter all the same. The beige didn't look that bad with my freckles, which I was thankful for. Pinks always made my face look like abstract art.

I reached down and touched my leg. I had taken extra time to shave my legs until they were smooth and silky. It was a little embarrassing to see how many freckles were on them, but what could be done at this point.

I had chosen a light green tank top and a plum colored pair of shorts. I checked myself out in the mirror and nodded at the overall effect. It was passable.

Downstairs, I pulled on a pair of sandals that I had bought at DSW in San Diego. They were cute Grecian looking with wraps up to my ankles. I was ready before Ky arrived and had a small bout of butterflies at the thought of going to his house as the car pulled up.

I knew he wasn't one to blow the horn and wait for me to come out, so I hurried on my way and hustled out the door, meeting him on the stairs to my porch.

I checked out his fit. He was in a pair of black and white plaid shorts that hung to just below his knees and a black T-shirt which made the gray in his eyes pop. I unabashedly checked him out before smiling at him and said, "You look *really* good!"

I was surprised when he blushed and looked down at his feet before glancing up and shyly saying, "Thank you. I think I should have been the one to say that to you though."

In the last week, I had seen Ky Linley be bashful, blush, and now, be awkward to the point of adorable. This was the same guy who had mowed through most of the who's who of upperclassmen and sophomores his sophomore year. I couldn't help but grin, when I realized that I was the one who had brought out all those sides of him. I had no clue as to what he was like in school, but he was cute as anything as far as I could see.

Of course, I also had to admit he was a freaking ten out of ten too!

When we got in his car, he was smiling. It was a gorgeous smile that made me think Trick's gleam was nothing compared to how hot AF this boy's lips were.

He sat back in the seat and rubbed his palms on his shorts. "I have to admit that I'm a little nervous about having you come over."

I laughed. "Why is that?" I asked.

He took a shaky breath and put the car in gear and reversed. "I never have girls over."

"Well, you still haven't. I'm coming over for Taylor," I ribbed him.

"True." He coughed.

"What about all the girls you... ahem, dated?" I asked. "And what about Shea?"

He bit his lips nervously and shook his head. "No. I've never had a girl come to my house. I used to always go to the girl's house... or I would meet them at a friend's house, parties sometimes. My mom was already sick by the time I started seeing Shea. It was never a good time for her to come over. She and I always went to her house. Her parents are never there. She has a shady uncle, but that's another conversation altogether."

I found it hard to believe considering he was the school stud. How could he notch his bedpost if he wasn't in his bed? "As a boy aren't you supposed to lure them back to your room to do dirty things with them? This hardly fits the image I had of you."

He swallowed and choked out another laugh. "Well, I won't lie. I got a lot of chances to lure girls places to do dirty things to them. But I didn't really ever want my mom to know what I was doing. I don't think she would really appreciate or approve of my activities and the amount of different girls that I had been doing them with. I knew she wouldn't approve of the type of girls I was doing, in any case. So why make trouble?"

"Are you telling me that your mom has never met any of your girlfriends?" I had a pretty hard time believing him.

"She met Shea. She came to a lot of my football and baseball games. But since we were on and off again so much... Well, I'll be real, I wasn't going to bring home someone who slept with me and two other guys in one night. Shea's a lot of things. She's not a bad person. She's looking for something in a person I can't be. I've offered my friendship, when she can take that..." He shrugged. "At the end of the day, I didn't want my parents to get caught up in Shea's dramas."

I gave him a hard look, narrowing my eyes at him. He looked at me and gave me a lopsided smile. "So what about me? Do you have second thoughts right now?"

He laughed. "Well to be fair, and you did remind me, I didn't invite you over, Taylor did. But I'm also sure that my mom is going to like you."

"So you're saying that I'm the type of girl you can take home to mama?" I said, trying not to smile.

He nodded and deadpanned. "Well, I'm not going to tell them that we are getting married right away. I think we should see one another for a little while before I pop the question. At least have one date behind us before I buy the ring. I would like to graduate before we start thinking of a family. But for right now, yeah, I'm thinking you're the kind of girl my mama is going to love."

I tried to stop the silly grin his words caused. I was going to be the first girl that met his parents at their house. We weren't even really dating yet. I mean, technically, we probably were by the definition of the word, but not by how we were defining it.

I stopped myself–what if I had this all wrong. What if he thought I was different in that his mom would just like me and *he* didn't invite me, *Taylor* had.

As if sensing my panic,, he poked me in the side and tilted his head my way. "There is something that I'm jealous about."

"Hmmm?" I felt the butterflies back.

He sighed. "How did my brother get a date before I did?"

I smiled. "I told you, this is a playdate. It's not a real date."

"You've said that but the thing is, you are still using the word 'date.' Please tell me you won't kiss my brother at the end of the night." His gray eyes sparkled at me.

"Well it really depends how the night goes. If I like him enough to come and play with him again some other time, I kind of think that is grounds for kissing at the end of the second date." I tapped my finger on the window frame, trying to appear cool.

"I'm going to store that factoid away. I'm a little sad that you like the shy, quiet types. I don't really fit the mold." He bit his lip.

I shook my head and leaned over and searched the radio for the college music station. I sat back satisfied when "It's Called: Freefall" by Paris Paloma came over the airwaves.

"I wouldn't say that I have a type. I'm open to all types. You have to remember my best friend is a gay Korean guy. We've talked a few times about the prospect of dating one another when the world seems cruel, and the boys we like let us down."

"The world is pretty cruel," Ky agreed. "I wonder if he would date me when I feel that way when a girl lets me down."

I laughed. "I'm sure he would find the hardship of smashing you easy to overcome despite your body count. I think he'd brave the rejection to see you without clothing on. When you texted me asking to send you a picture of me without a top on in ninth grade, he told me to ask you to go first."

Ky flinched and his face tightened. "I was a fucking

piece of shit to you back then. I'm sorry, Jace. So sorry. If you want pictures of me, you can have anything you want. I owe you so much for what you had to go through because of me. Hell, he can have a photo of me, and he can tell everyone he and I are dating and then Gaven can have the heat off him."

I was going to apologize for setting him off, but my mom's words from yesterday about not being an apologist morning rang in my head, and I swallowed it back.

We slowed down in front of a pretty, large, yellow and green house that looked almost Victorian.

"Is this where you live?" My eyes must have been comically wide.

He nodded, pulling into a driveway next to a custom built, blue Jeep Gladiator Mojave. Ky worked constantly and said his family needed money, but both the house and vehicle said otherwise. "What do your parents do for a living?"

"My dad is an architect, and my mom had her own interior design business before she got sick. She sold it, and stays at home now. They used to build and design homes for people who wanted something one of a kind. My dad still does it, but he lost the professional consulting end my mom once added." He stopped the car and put it in park and put the parking brake on. "You ready for this?"

"No." I shook my head looking around. My mom works at a pub, and my dad got by on a tenured professor's salary until he screwed that up. Ky's home was way out of my league.

He walked around while I sat there and opened the car door. When we made it to the entrance of his house, he turned to me and swallowed. I could see he was as nervous as I was. I reached out his hand and gave it a squeeze. He nodded once and opened the door.

The inside was beautiful. It had really high ceilings and real wooden floors. The entryway was papered a royal blue on top and the lower part was wood panels, which were painted white.

"The family room is this way," he said, moving further into the house.

The scent of the house was nice. It was floral and reminded me of Frangipani. The family room was carpeted in egg shell color, and the walls were painted a nutmeg. Around the room were photos of Sophie, Taylor and Ky at different ages. One wall had three pieces of art that looked like it had been done by a small child. I moved closer to them. "Those are finger paintings we did as children. The one on the left in blue and green is mine."

"You know what you were doing in this one. Your command space and use of color speaks to the soul of the pain and trials of preschool," I said, pretending to critique it.

"I know it was one of my most sought after pieces. I disappointed a lot of those who were fans of my finger painting when I gave it to my mom to hang on the refrigerator." He smirked.

I moved around the room looking at the different photos. As I saw the photos of Ky at different ages, I couldn't help but notice that he had a really awkward period when he was thin and long limbed. I don't remember him that way though, he was always just the boy I loved. Although, having gotten to know him, I knew it was infatuation back then. I was barely getting to really know him now.

"Hello there, there appears to be a young woman in my home. The Earth must be revolving backwards. Should I look outside? Are pigs in flight?" a husky woman's voice said, and I turned to meet the owner. She was looking at us with an arched brow but a kind cant to her head. "Are you going to do introductions, Carter Kyrin? I didn't raise you to be rude."

Ky blushed, and my eyes nearly popped out of my head. Ky's full name was Carter Kyrin? I hadn't known that! And I didn't know if I would ever get used to the school stud blushing!

"Mom, this is Jacelyn. Jace, this is my mom, Sandra Ann-Elizabeth." He moved a few steps closer to me and started to chuckle. "And I'm not too old to get spanked according to her and that is her you're-going-to-get-it look"

I glanced up to find her also red cheeked and shaking her head ruefully. "My son is rude. It's nice to finally meet you. My son's talked a lot about you."

"Likewise!" I choke out over a lump of nerves in my throat. "You have a lovely family, and your home is just... there are no words."

Sandra smiled, and I noticed that Sophie looked a lot like her. They both had delicate cheekbones and arching brows that were a little darker than their hair. Sandra was elegant even though she was wearing a blue silk tank-top that fit just under her breasts and flared around her waist.

"You know you're a first. Ky's never brought one of his girlfriends home before." She tried not to smile but instead just looked impish.

Ky's face tightened at the word girlfriend. He was obviously uncomfortable by his mother's use of it. I reached out and squeezed his hand again, as a way of telling him I was okay with what she said. His shoulders relaxed.

"Are you okay with ham? We are having a roast for dinner tonight." She stepped back toward a room I suspected was the kitchen.

"Jace is a vegetarian." Ky came to my rescue, and I grimaced.

"Oh! I was vegetarian in college. I can make a quick veggie casserole." She smiled broadly.

"You don't have to do that." I insisted with a shake of my head.

"Please, stay," she pleaded.

Ky rolled his eyes. "My mom wants to interrogate you. Mom, just so you know, I was late to the game. I didn't even get a chance to invite her over. It was Taylor's doing. She has a playdate with him tonight. He's going to teach her to play video games."

I opened my mouth to defend myself but couldn't, so I closed it and felt a blush fill my cheeks. "It's true."

Sandra laughed. "Well, he hasn't brought home a girl-friend either."

"She's not his girlfriend!" Ky argued.

"If she's not, whose is she?" his mom teased more.

Ky fumbled, and grabbed my hand to pull me to him. "I'm going to show her the house."

"Your brother's in his room, Ky. Tell him to keep his door open with his–" his mom needled.

I tried not to laugh as Ky pulled me upstairs and into his room. "You know she's nothing but trouble." He sat down on the end of his bed and buried his head in his hands. "Maybe this was a mistake."

I looked around and found a computer chair and sat in it. The walls of his room were deep green on three walls and one striped accent wall. There was one window, and it was double sized with a window seat. I was surprised by all the bookshelves and books. I had no idea he was a reader. I was learning so much about him during this visit.

I couldn't help it, my eyes moved back to him on his

bed. It was made, neatly put together, it had to be a queen. A large bed. "If this is too difficult, you can take me home. We don't have to do this."

"No." He looked up. "I want you here. I'm nervous. She made it worse. I'm not the same guy at home as I am outside, and I'm worried that you won't like what you see here. First of all, I'm my mom's bitch in jokes apparently."

I laughed. "It wasn't that bad! I had no idea your name was Carter Kyrin. Is that top secret?"

"Well, teacher's know, so not really. I'm named after my dad, we don't call me Carter because my mom would be confused as to which one of us she was putting in the dog house," he quipped.

"So this real you, do you sin and sacrifice animals in Satanic Rites?" I popped an eyebrow up in question.

He laughed. "Not in a while."

"See, you can't be that bad. You're reformed." I looked around his room. "So are you supposed to have a girl in your room with your door closed?"

"Considering I'm not planning to be forward with you, you and my mom can settle your concern." He sat back and leaned on his arms. "I'm not kissing you until after our first date, no matter how much you look like you want me to."

"Do I look like that?" I put my hands to my face.

He was quiet for a while, then broke the silence. "I'm really happy that you are here."

"I am too, Ky. I'm flattered that you are letting me see this other side of you, even if I'm not sure why I'm here if you aren't comfortable."

He looked down with a pained look on his face, and I heard him mutter. "You don't know why I want you with me. That's great. I suck at this."

"The tour?" I reminded him because it was time to lighten the topic.

"Well, this is my room."

I looked around more. I noticed everything was tidy. My eyes went back to the bookcase, and I got up and walked to it.

"I didn't realize you were a reader. I mean, I assume you've read these, and they aren't just for show." I pursed my lips and skimmed the titles with my fingertip.

When he didn't answer right away, I looked over my shoulder. His lips were quirked up. It was different from his normal smile, and it was hard for me to get a read on it. "I read. I like the classics: Steinbeck, Victor Hugo, Hemingway, F. Scott Fitzgerald, Edgar Allan Poe..."

I nodded and pulled out a leather bound collection of sonnets by Shakespeare. "So you aren't just a pretty face?"

He looked away, blushing again. "I do very well in school, and it's not just that I test well. I didn't skip a grade though unlike some people." He made a point to give me a sly smile making sure I knew he was referring to me.

I smiled. "No, you didn't. I guess I'm just better than you."

"I know you are. You've taught me a lot, and you don't even know it," he said quietly.

I didn't like how serious he sounded. I didn't want him to get too introspective and down. I gave him a tilt of my head and a saucy wink. "Well, maybe it's time for you to teach me a thing or two."

His eyebrows rose, and he sat up. "This sounds promising. Talk. What are we doing?"

"You want to give me a tutorial on the game your brother wants to play?" I pointed to his computer.

"What do I get for it?" He put his hands on his knees and raised his eyes to me in question.

"I'll buy you dinner," I bartered.

He laughed. "Now, I feel like you're trying to buy my affections."

"They do say the way to a man's heart is through his stomach," I joked as I went to sit next to him. His eyes dropped to my lips before quickly rising back up to meet mine. "Will you go out on a date with me?" I asked, all joking put aside.

"When?" He bit his lip.

"After work tomorrow night?" I whispered.

"Can't." He sighed and squeezed his eyes shut in apparent pain. "I have a final coming up, and I need to come home and sleep. I was going to tell you."

I nodded. "Next week sometime?"

"Definitely." He looked at my lips again and leaned over and gently kissed my cheek. "I'm dying to take you out."

There was a knock on the door as we stared at one another, and Ky pulled back and cleared his throat. "It's open."

Taylor pushed it open. "Mom said we should come down to dinner. After that, we are going to play *Among Us* with some online friends."

And just like that the bubble that Ky and I were in popped, with it the butterflies from my stomach flew free, and my racing heart turned to nervous adrenaline.

I stood when he did and followed him downstairs. He was different here, and I just wanted to spend more time here with him, because this Ky was someone that I could actually fall for all over again.

seventeen

· · ·

"RICKY, can I take a fifteen minute break to talk to Peter?" I yelled back to him.

It was Thursday, and Peter had texted me before work upset because of Gaven. Peter finally bore his soul to me yesterday before I went to work which made me late, which in turn made Ky late too. Then today, he saw Gaven kissing Ashley Keating before French in the junior hall.

Sometimes I wish I hadn't homeschooled. I apparently missed the classroom gossip and lunch period drama. Peter and Sophie both gave her a set down when she tried to nose in on talking to them when they were confronting Gaven in the cafeteria.

"Take your break, and when you come back, I want you to cover Melissa until Ky returns from his delivery," Ricky instructed. I thanked him and headed out to the parking lot where Peter sat teary-eyed in his car.

He handed me a Mickey-D's sweet tea, no ice, and reached over to hug me, setting his head on my shoulder. "Men suck."

I held him for a moment then pushed him back. "Tell

159

me what happened," I demanded, turning and leaning against the passenger door to give him my full attention.

"Gaven is a class-A jerk. He's been telling me he can't come out. I was fine with that." He grabbed a tissue out of his console and blew his nose. "Not everyone is comfortable with coming out. It's something you have to do when it feels right. But when you do it, you're looked at differently. I didn't mind keeping us low-key. But on Monday, someone apparently joked with Gaven that something he did was totally homo.

"It was a jock, and they say those things just to say 'em, and let's be honest–half those guys have tendencies and can't deal with their curiosity. But in this case, Gav got para-noid that someone was onto him. He told me Tuesday that he needed time to think. The next day, he blew me off then today, he's making out with Ashley. Rumor is, he fucking slipped into her DMs last night. He's a jackass."

"What a dick," I sympathized, because that was my line when something like that happens. The best friend code insists I say it. Once a guy steps on a best friend's heart, it is open season to bash the bastard. Peter knew the code, and he looked up, smiling at me sadly.

"I don't know why I'm so hurt over it. We weren't exclusive, and we were barely anything at all. He never said anything that led me on. It didn't bother me that he denied being gay, but it bothers me that he denies being my friend now. He did things to me that were a whole lot more than what friends should do to one another; we crossed that platonic line into intimate territory." Peter sniffled.

I grabbed his hand and squeezed. "What did Sophie say?"

"She said, and I quote, 'fuck him, he doesn't deserve a

good thing until he can be a good thing.'" Peter wiped his eyes.

"Hallelujah, sister, and amen!" I said, holding up my hands in praise.

Peter cracked another reluctant smile.

"I know it doesn't help how you feel, but being different isn't something everyone is cut out to do. *You've* embraced it, you always have. I love you for being so uncompromising and strong. But not everyone is as incredible as you. And there are some fish out there you just have to throw back. But it doesn't mean that you need to pack up your rod and go home. You can't stop fishing just because of one bad fish. You gotta keep going until you get your prize." I leaned forward and squeezed his arm.

Peter chuckled and shook his head ruefully. "Oh, I don't think you have to worry. I am not going to 'pack up my rod' over Gaven Martins. He didn't ruin *that* for me."

I ignored that and asked him. "So what do you want to do next?

We had made a deal years ago when Ky demolished my reputation that we wouldn't let one another dwell on shitty things that happened. We would always try to keep each other looking to the future and find a way to move forward.

He inhaled deeply and looked out the windshield, "Well, short term, I want a calzone. Further out, I want to go to a spa and be pampered for a day. I could get my hair done, get a manicure, the works, then I can show Gaven just how much hotter I am than Ashley. Because, dammit! I am!"

"Well, let's do it then! Saturday. I'll get someone to cover me, and we can end the day with mocktails at my house," I declared with a clap of my hands.

Peter nodded. "Do you think we can invite Sophie? I've

been sitting with her, Taylor and..." he mumbled, "...at lunch. She's really–"

"Wait, what did you mumble?" I teased and pressed my lips together so as not to smile. I knew who he was sitting with, but I wanted him to say it.

He sighed and mumbled again, trying to avoid admitting what we both knew.

I shook my head and sang, "Nope, can't hear you."

"KY!" Alright? KY! I've been sitting with your boy toy at lunch! His sister is really funny. She's been playing the imaginary conversation game with me when we hang out. She's as good at it as you are." He sighed then dropped his head. "Oh God. I've been sitting with Ky...sorry I didn't tell you sooner. I thought, Mr. Nice-Looking-In-Jeans would tell you."

I burst out laughing. "He's good at keeping other people's secrets. I would love for Sophie to come. Do you want to call her and invite her or should I?

Peter dug out his phone and started texting. "I got it. Thanks, Jace. You're the best sorta hag."

"As long as you aren't looking for a beard, I'm your girl!" I looked at my phone and sighed. "I have to get back inside."

"Let's hope you never have to be a beard." Peter raised his hand for a high-five.

I gave him a high five before I returned to work. Ky came back inside when there was only ten minutes left of Melissa's lunch, and I happened to be listening to "They Don't Love It" by Jack Harlow.

"What is this noise?" he asked, cringing.

I snorted. "Well, this is what the kids listen to these days."

"Whatever." He tossed down his keys on the little shelf

we had for odds and ends and turned to me and hummed. "So, about that da–"

"Wait!" I held up a hand. I hadn't talked to him about my mom's invitation yet, but right now, I needed to focus on preparing the pizza I was tasked with.

He came up next to me and grabbed the ticket I was working on. "I think you are forgetting pepperoncinis."

"You're just trying to mess with me. I know they don't go on this pizza." I finished it up by adding mushrooms, and grimaced; I hated mushrooms. "How was your delivery?"

"Mr. Marshall gave me a two dollar and fifteen cent tip on a seventy dollar order to Lake Ballant." Ky reported. Mr. Marshall was the economics teacher at FHS. He was known to be really cheap.

"Why do we deliver so far out?" I muttered.

"Because Ricky wants to beat our competitors with our delivery options," Ky said and poked me in the side. "Move over. I'm taking over the orders and music."

"So..." I started as I moved out of his way.

He looked up, his eyes following me. "So?"

"My mom asked me to invite you over tomorrow afternoon. She's kicking Maris out, it will just be the three of us. Will you come over after you get out of school?"

Ky's head canted to the side. "Your mom is asking me out?"

I saw where I went wrong with my invitation and bit my lip. "My mom asked to meet you, Ky. I'm inviting you to come over. I want you to come over," I reiterated the last part to make things clearer.

He gave me a quizzical look. Was it really that difficult to decide to come meet my mom? Maybe he was worried about Maris' reaction.

Finally, he gave a singular nod. "Yes."

He didn't say anything else on the subject, but there was a giddy feeling of anticipation that carried through the next five minutes of silence.

I held the refrigerator door open as I moved things around and felt the door tug out of my hand.

"Hey, before you interrupt or distract me again..." he started. "I want to take you out on a date this Sunday."

"A real date?" I asked. "Where we finally kiss at the end?" I said in a low voice.

"I was thinking something like that, yeah." He nodded. He looked nervous. "So do you want to go?"

I swallowed, letting out a shaky breath. "I really do, but I just switched days with Mikey, so I can go out and have a gal date with Peter on Saturday."

"We can go earlier in the day before work," Ky said.

I bit my lip and nodded.

His lips twitched and Melissa came back in, ignoring us and switched the music from Ky's choice to her normal station. Missy Elliot's "Work It" was playing. Melissa whooped and started dancing and singing along. Ky closed his eyes, as his shoulders started shaking with laughter. "I love this woman. She's the best thing about this place."

I nodded in agreement. "I thought she was mean when I first started here but she was just all business."

He shook his head. "Nope, she's a goofball and the best sort of weirdo."

Melissa wiggled her hips. "You think you can handle this badonka-donk-donk..."

ThatPizzaKy: Should I be bringing anything?

Me: No. Just bring yourself. I'm cooking lunch.

ThatPizzaKy: I'll be there in fifteen minutes.

My mom was trying to help me make lunch when in actuality, she was getting in my way while I was trying to get everything ready. She had more of a Kraft Mac & Cheese type of cooking style, so it really impressed her that I had taken to cooking from scratch..

However, sometimes she got a bee up her bum and thought something I was making didn't 'sound' right to her, so she would go and 'fix it.' It was a real pain in the butt.

Thankfully, today wasn't one of those days. She was just excited about meeting Ky. I decided to make spanako-pita, which she referred to as spinach pies, and they were one of her favorites.

"Will he like iced tea, or should I open a bottle of Coke?" she asked, puttering around nervously.

"I think whatever we have will be fine. He's not too picky." I smiled at her reassuringly. I couldn't afford to have butterflies today when my mom was just as anxious. One of us had to hold it together.

She rubbed her hands together. "This is so exciting. You're finally bringing home a boy who likes girls. It's like my baby is all grown up."

I gave her a dry look. Her jokes were good, I just didn't want her so busy entertaining that she forgot she was supposed to be seeing if she approved of Ky.

When Ky arrived and knocked at the door, we looked at one another and grinned. She rubbed her hands together with excitement. "Do I open it, or do you?"

"I've got it!" I said. "You stay here and practice your lines."

She nodded and in a gruff voice she said, "Just what *are* your intentions with my daughter, young man!?"

I rolled my eyes at her and headed to the front door.

I opened the door and found Ky was dressed in shorts again and wore a t-shirt that read, "Wanted: Dead or Alive, Schrödinger's Cat." I motioned for him to come inside. He didn't look nervous, which was a change from the trip we had made to his house.

"My mom is in the kitchen. She is gathering steam, so she can be amusing and say things that will rival the top comedians," I warned.

Ky smiled. "I really like Will Farrell. I hope she can do impersonations too."

"Don't let her hear that. She will be giving it the old college try in no time." I shook my head and led the way.

My mom greeted him with a smile. "I *do* remember you. You were at so many of Maris' parties growing up. You are so handsome now."

I burst out laughing at the blush that flushed his cheeks and passed my mom to check the spanakopita. "Nice job making him embarrassed. That will make him feel at home."

"Well, I can embarrass you, and you will feel like equals," she said brightly.

I cringed.

Ky laughed. "I haven't been here since eighth grade. It was the year Maris had the One Direction cake. I imagine she's not as thrilled by that fact now as she was then."

My mom nodded. "Don't tell anyone, but even though we didn't have a party for her freshman year, Jacie and I got her a Justin Bieber cake to celebrate. Maris is sort of terminally tuned to pop music."

Ky grinned. "I think that is why I get the plain, no frills, cakes. I don't want them to come back and plague me later."

I relaxed. My mom got along with almost everyone. She couldn't be called a true extrovert because she really needed her alone time to recharge, but she could socialize as if it was an innate talent.

I served the spanakopita and poured drinks while they talked.

"So, you will be graduating in a few weeks. That must feel good? Will you be having a graduation party?" my mom asked.

"It feels a bit strange to think I'm finishing up high school. Don't get me wrong, I'm ready to get out. It just seems weird to think that I won't be returning to Fellsdale School District in the fall," Ky admitted, and my mom nodded in understanding.

I didn't, but my mom and Ky were more institutionalized than I was I guess. Homeschooling had done something for me, and it had been to give me a world without walls. I hadn't had a classroom or a schedule created by someone other than me in two years. I just put my mind to it and plugged away at it: morning, noon and night. I went to museums, read books and often was my own freaking tutor.

"Where do you plan to go to college, Ky?" My mom sipped her tea.

Ky swallowed his pie and nodded. "I'm going to state. I want to stay close to home. I had some scholarships, but my mom's been sick. I don't want to go too far away to go to school. I don't mind dorming, but I want to be close enough to drive home on weekends."

"Maris and Jacelyn are both going to state. I'm a little worried about how Maris will find the discipline to stick with something like college. I think the only reason she goes to high school is to socialize with Alex. When left to her own devices, I think she will debate the finer points of mochas over literature then eventually answer the call to Starbucks." My mom looked at me and pointed my way. "And when that happens, you let her go. She has to crash and burn without her sister saving her butt."

My lips flattened. Despite our current fight I didn't like the idea that Mare should be left to sink when I could help her swim the deep waters of college. I chose not to debate against it for the moment though and merely lifted a shoulder in a half shrug. "You can't really deny the power of a mocha."

My mom shook her head. "I guess, for some. Mochas seem so conformist though, Jacie. Strive for more. I want you kids to get up in rascally things. I haven't ever got a chance to pick you up from anywhere interesting yet."

I looked at Ky and concluded. "My mom would prefer picking me up at the police station as opposed to Starbucks."

He chuckled. "Maris thinks that I'm a bad influence. Should I worry she's going to lead me into a life of crime? Playing ding dong dash in Fellsdale? Mugging people in Maystown for mocha money?"

My mom clapped her hands excitedly, then rubbed them together. "Now we're talking. Jacie promised me underage drinking. Do you have a fake ID?"

"No, ma'am. But I will happily get one, if it pleases you." Ky played along.

"You have to let a little five o'clock shadow grow in. Mess up your hair a bit." She narrowed her eyes as he ran his hands through his hair before she widened her eyes. "Oh goodness, Ky! You're better looking than Alex!"

Ky laughed and blushed.

"Okay, mom! I'm putting my foot down. No more flirting with the guy I'm dating." I exhaled and rapped my knuckles on the table.

She shrugged and gestured at him. "I can't deny what the University of My Eyes see, Jacelyn. You picked a good looking guy for a boyfriend!"

Now Ky couldn't even look up from the ground. I wanted to tape her mouth shut. We hadn't used those terms, because we hadn't gotten that far yet. I wanted to die beside him on the bonfire my mom had started.

"So mom, how's the spanakopita?" I said, diverting the conversation.

"The spinach pies are really good, Jacie. I think that they are going to be better after they sit in the refrigerator for a day. The Phyllo dough will get a little softer, then the crumbs won't get all over all over the place." My mom licked her finger and pressed it to a crumb on her plate before sticking it in her mouth.

I nodded my agreement and looked at Ky to see how he was doing and found him giving me a soft smile.

"What do you do at Piero's, Ky?" A crumb dropped in her lap, and she brushed it onto the floor where I would have to clean it up later–this house was so assbackwards as far as responsibilities and chores.

Ky inhaled. "I'm the delivery guy and Jack-of-All-Trades. I also make..." The conversation took off from there, and my mom continued to ask questions that stayed on safe ground until we had to go to work.

Unlike my sister, my mom took the time to really get to know him, and by the time I was gathering my things, my mom was inviting him over again on her next day off.

"I'll cook!" she promised. I turned and gave her a shake of my head to nip that idea in the bud.

When we got in the car and got our seat belts on, it was quiet. Ky sat there for a moment then cracked up laughing. I looked at him like he'd lost his mind.

"Jacelyn, your mom is awesome. She's fantastic! And just so you know, it's okay with me that she called me your boyfriend. I like the status upgrade." He started laughing again. "Even if your mom gave it to me, and you didn't."

"Whatever, you clown. You haven't even kissed me," I grumbled. "You get boyfriend status when you seal the deal by putting your lips on mine. Now drive."

eighteen

. . .

"ARE WE PICKING UP SOPHIE?" I asked, getting into Peter's car.

He seemed to be in better spirits today. I had spoken to him at two this morning when I had gotten home from work. He hadn't talked about Gaven, only about the plans we had for today.

He nodded and grabbed his phone to fiddle with his Amazon Music App. "Maroon" by Taylor Swift started playing. He sighed happily and looked at me. "Today is going to be so good."

"It will be." I nodded.

"We are going to go get Sophie now. Did you make appointments at the spa?" he asked.

"Yes, I wouldn't let you down." I looked out the window as a white Subaru WRX STI passed us. Such a sexy car.

We drove to the Linleys. When we arrived, I got out and went to the door. Sandra opened the door, and her eyes widened, she opened her arms as an invitation to hug her. I squeezed her gently, her slight frame felt delicate.

"It's so good to see you again, Jacelyn. I think you've

won over each one of my children. Taylor might want another playdate. He's been talking about how hopeless you are at games, and I think he liked that. Ky's in love. And now you and Peter are taking Sophie with you for the day. It's nice that you're impartial," she said, jokingly.

Sophie came flying down the stairs with Ky following. He was dressed in a T-shirt and sweatpants. He looked rumpled, really sleepy and good. I wanted to take a picture and post the thirst trap on all my social media, so I could brag about the quality I was dating.

He waved at me, but we didn't get to talk as his sister stepped up to her mom and kissed her on the cheek. "We will be back tonight!"

Sandra held her back from taking off. "Do you have money?"

"Yes." Sophie nodded.

"And your phone, Soph? Tell me you have your phone, in case you need to call me for something."

She held up her phone and smiled. "I didn't forget it this time. And before you ask, the plan is that we go to the spa, then we are going back to Jace's to have mocktails and watch rom-coms and hate-talk men. Her number is on the fridge. Everything is going to be okay."

"Hate-talk men?" Ky asked, coming closer to the entry.

I laughed, shaking my head. "One man."

Sophie shook her head. "All men, and we are starting with you, doofus." She ran for the car.

Sandra got a worried look on her face. "Sophie! For Heaven's sake, don't run! Jacelyn, let me know if she needs to come home sooner."

I nodded with a smile. I looked over at Ky, as he waved and turned to go back upstairs, yelling, "Text me later, Jace!"

As I got back in the car, sliding in the backseat now, I tugged one of Sophie's curls. "Give, what's the deal?" I am dying to hear why her mom is so protective.

"I don't mention friends. We don't invite people over, and I hardly go out." She exhaled. "We are a family of social misfits."

"Your brother wasn't always like that," Peter said.

"My brother is a lot of things you don't know about," she said protectively, shutting up Peter. "We don't want to give mom anything to stress over. It was really hard when she was first diagnosed. Cancer runs in our family on her side. She has gone through chemo, we thought she beat it, but it came back. She had surgery and radiation, and thought that was it, and it was metastasized.

"We are never going to be able to be crazy and cause trouble because that stress isn't something she can take, and it will be time wasted away from her. Why rebel? She means too much to us. Plus, what happens at home is private. It's not for the rest of the world to know."

Having listened to the speech Sophie gave, Peter asked the question I was dying to know. "So, why are you telling us?"

She smiled like the Mona Lisa. "My older brother's in love with Jace, and I have it on good authority from my younger brother that she's different. As for why I'm telling you, Peter... you already told me that I'm going to be your new hag. I feel that I owe you a little trust. Especially since you've given me your own."

Twice in ten minutes a member of the Linley family had professed Ky's love for me. I hoped it was true and not a cruel exaggeration. Still, I told myself to assume it was the latter and not read too much into it.

I cleared my throat. "Anyone hear news from or about Gaven this morning?"

Sophie's shoulders fell. "He's taking Ashley to see some adaptation of *Midsummer Night's Dream* at the Catholic College in Clarkston."

I rolled my eyes. "And he wonders why people have started piecing together he's gay."

Sophie and Peter both chuckled.

"Well, eff him," Sophie said loudly. "When I go out with a gay guy, I want people to know it!"

I watched Peter's face in the mirror as it softened and his eyes sparkled. He appreciated Sophie's comment. I knew a lot of girls stayed away from Peter at school. I didn't understand what they thought would rub off on them. But they treated him like he was contagious. Or worse, some would be nice to his face and tear him down behind his back to talk themselves up around guys.

I wasn't going to be around next year, neither was Ky, and I was glad these two had found one another–even if this was early days.

"Do your parents know Peter is gay?" I asked.

"Yeah. I told them before we all went out to the movies. My mom doesn't care. When she went to college, she had a good friend who was gay. He studied interior design with her. A few years ago, before she got sick, we all went to see him get married. It was very cool." She reached out and patted Peter's shoulder. "I promise that Ted had a few Gavens before he met Ethan."

"When I get married, I'm going to make you and Jace my Maidens of Honor." Peter smiled.

"I think you're getting ahead of yourself, Peter Kim. I still have hope that I won't still be a maiden on your wedding day."

Sophie looked over her shoulder and grinned. "I know for a fact that if my brother wasn't trying so hard not to screw things up, he would rectify that problem quickly."

I felt myself blush. "Your brother hasn't even kissed me yet." I sighed with disappointment.

"WHAT!?" Sophie and Peter both gasped at the same time.

"I am serious. He hasn't kissed me." I looked out the window as we entered Maystown.

"Sophie has the inside scoop," Peter said. "Tell me, what are his intentions? Why isn't he putting the moves all over her? Has the dog really changed his spots?"

"You sound like my mother with all your questions, and you are mixing your metaphors. I don't think we should talk about this," I said.

Sophie ignored me. "My brother's gone on her completely. He's had a crush on her for a long time. We are talking about elephant years, and this is a dream come true to him to get her to give him a second look. He had a picture of her at some dance on the mirror in his room forever and took it down when she was coming over. And when she started working at Piero's, he started coming home late. My dad gave him an earful. Ky finally told them about her. It's the first time he's ever talked about bringing a girl home." She laughed. "But then Taylor invited her over before Ky got a chance."

I knew for a fact my face was beet red. I was mortified and happy all at once. Peter wasn't done though. "So, he isn't looking just to smash her?"

"I mean he definitely wants that to be part of it, but they apparently have a complicated situationship. He uses words for her like *different, special, unlike everyone else*. She's totally his BAE. My opinion? She's the one. He's dead serious." Sophie sucked her lips making a smacking sound.

"Alright you two." I slapped the mid console. "I'm right here. We have talked about this enough. We should change the subject."

Sophie ignored me again, turning to Peter, she read-justed her seatbelt and narrowed her eyes. "What about Jace? What are her intentions? Believe it or not, my brother is delicate with his emotions. He's never given his heart away before."

I raised my voice, "EXCUSE ME!"

Peter shook his head and replied. "Totally on the up and up. She's been head over heels for him since grade school. She wouldn't believe he was talking trash freshman year, when he was saying it in front of her. She was his biggest defender and made cow eyes at him for the remainder of the year, despite him doing her dirty. And OMG! You should have seen them at Jimmy's party when they first saw one another when she got back. I thought the house was going up in flames."

I kicked Peter's seat. "I'm getting out and walking at the next stop if you two don't stop. I don't think this is either of your business."

Peter turned around briefly and looked at me. "You wanted me to give him a fair shot, and Sophie just totally swayed me to your side. I'm on the Ky train. I'm headed to Kyville."

"Shut up, Peter!" I said, defensively now. I slammed my head into the headrest behind me and growled. "I know today was supposed to be for you, but I would really appreciate it if it wasn't at my expense."

We pulled into the salon and got out. Sophie wrapped

her arms around me. "Don't get so upset. We kid, because we love."

Peter joined us and wrapped us both in his arms. "We love, because we can kid."

We hadn't made an appointment for it, but once Lynnette heard Peter's failed love affair, she started babying her favorite client. Peter was immediately treated to a shoulder rub by Magda while Lynnette did his pedicure.

"This is the life!" Peter relaxed.

"Do you want waxing?" Magda asked, scrunching her face. "No offense, but your brow and face could use a clean up."

"My face!" he gasped. "Honestly? Is my upper lip unsightly?"

I ignored the rest of the conversation and went with Sue to have my own wax job. I was getting a first. Eyebrows, legs, armpits and bikini wax. I won't delve into it too much other than to say, it was a long process, and Sue saw parts of me that no one other than my lady doctor had seen.

"Jace, I picked out colors for your pedicure!" Sophie said, brightly waving a bottle in the air. It was called Metallic Mermaid since it was a blue-green color.

I nodded in approval. "I love it."

"You can pick out a second color for your manicure." She pointed behind us.

I studied the selection and looked down at the one in my hand. "Nah, I like this. I'll do it for both."

When we finished at the spa, we went to the mall, and passed by Electric Waves, when Peter's feet slowed. "You know...?"

I arched my brow. "Well if you know, you know," I answered.

"I clearly don't know." Sophie looked back and forth between us in confusion.

I pursed my lips. "Peter wants to change his hairstyle."

Sophie bit her lip. "Well, let's see if they can do it!"

She headed in and walked right up to the desk before she came back. "They have a new girl who just got out of school with no one on her books, but the girl is apparently a little edgy."

Peter's eyes sparkled. "You two shop. I'm going to get my hair fixed."

Sophie and I went on a spending spree and returned an hour and half later when we got a text from Peter. He was sitting outside, and my eyes widened. "PETER KIM!"

"I'm next!" Sophie ran inside.

"Connie's going to have a fit." I grabbed him by the chin. He had a shorter version of his usual haircut but with a shock of pink along the front right side going back..

"The hairstylist can take me. I'm not getting color, just a cut. I'll be done sooner than Peter, but they have another slot open... come with, Jace!" Sophie said, her eyes sparkling.

We were escorted to opposite sides of the salon, and I couldn't see her. I worried she'd go overboard, and Sandra and Carter would kill me.

The woman who handled me snapped her fingers in front of me to get my attention, and I apologized. "I'm so sorry. But my friends' parents are going to kill me."

An hour later, I was waiting with Peter having had my hair cut into long layers to frame my face, when Sophie walked out. Her black hair had been cut short into an acute bob, with a high fringe framing her eyes. She looked adorable in a goth-emo way.

As we left the mall, Peter kept checking his phone.

"What are you doing?" I asked him.

He sighed. "I posted the look on Insta and Tok. I got tons of likes, but Gaven Insta'd me. Dirty puke."

It was a quiet ride back to my place. Gaven had undone all the work we'd managed to do with a little flaming. I hated him, and I had never met him.

We let Peter order the movie we were going to watch from Amazon. It was ridiculous, and the requisite grand gesture was taking place when Mare came in and slammed the door. "What the hell have you done to yourself?" she asked, appalled.

"You don't like it noona?" He gave her his most winning smile and raised his virgin mojito.

She stomped over and grabbed his chin. "Peter, your mother and father are going to absolutely shit bricks."

"Are you saying that it might get me some attention?" He winked.

"What in God's name would make you do that?" She shook her head, troubled.

"A lot of Manga." He then sighed. "Kpop too. Specifically, J-Hope?"

My sister snorted. "Oh, don't blame it on him. I'm positive he can't save you."

Sophie, not understanding the reference, asked, "Who?"

Before Peter could explain I hopped in. "J-Hope is a Kpop idol Peter loves. From BTS. He has a big thing for him. Personally, I like V."

"Show me!" Sophie demanded. Peter pointed at me, and I got up to go get my laptop. I could hear Sophie and Peter talking to my sister in the other room and was happy to hear Mare being cordial. Every few comments, my sister made an exclamation about Peter's hair. I silently seconded her. His parents were going to have cows.

When I came back, Peter grabbed the laptop and did a Google search. Their heads leaned in together as they started looking at the members of BTS. I got up to clean and occasionally commented but allowed them to have some bonding time. My sister watched all of us. She finally went over and sat down on Peter's opposite side and joined them, and I walked into the kitchen to start cleaning up the glasses and the drink items we had used. Mocktails were sixty percent sugar, and the counter was sticky as all get out.

My phone chimed, and I grabbed it from my purse and smiled when I saw it was Ky texting me.

> ThatPizzaKy: It's 11:12. Is there any chance my sister is coming home tonight. *winky face emoji*

Me: I sort of think Peter and Sophie should live with me for a while.

> ThatPizzaKy: Are things going that well?

Me: *Sad face emoji* They both got haircuts today and I think your parents will disown her. Peter's parents definitely will. I just have to have hope that both parental units understand how little control I have over Poppy and Branch.

> ThatPizzaKy: *Shock face emoji* You better send me a picture.

> ThatPizzaKy: Who are Poppy and Branch?

Me: You know, the main characters from
The Trolls movies. You'll understand when I
send the picture.

I walked back into the living room and stood in front of the trio, who were now arguing over the perfection of Matthew Daddario. "Smile!" I sang. I snapped a picture and found my sister was actually smiling.

I sent the picture to Ky as I walked back to the kitchen.

ThatPizzaKy: Wow. She looks really
mature. I don't know if I like that.

Me: What are your parents going to say?

ThatPizzaKy My mom will probably want to
go get hers done the same way. She'll love
it. My dad will want to go get a new hobby
so he doesn't obsess over the fateful day
when she brings home a boy.

That made me laugh. I had hoped that they would have good reactions over it.

ThatPizzaKy: Can you tell her that dad
wants her to come home. She's been
ignoring his texts.

I stuck my head into the other room. "Soph, you and Peter need to wrap things up. Your dad wants you home."

Peter looked up. "Can I sleep here tonight?"

I nodded. "Yeah. I think that's a good idea."

Maris snorted. "For the rest of your life." She got up and headed upstairs.

As Sophie grabbed her things, I leaned against the wall and watched them tease one another. I felt a bittersweet knot in my chest. He needed this, but a part of me felt like I was losing a part of him.

He ran over and kissed my forehead. "Be back in a bit."

"Thanks, Jacelyn. Have fun tomorrow." She hugged me and kissed my cheek. "We love you!"

I watched them pull out.

> Me: Peter is driving Sophie home now. Are we still going out tomorrow?

> ThatPizzaKy: Are you backing out on me?

> Me: *Smiley face emoji* Nope. Just nervous.

> ThatPizzaKy: I'll be over to get you at 9. We can spend the entire morning on the trails. Don't wear sandals, make sure you wear socks with your Keds and bring a sweatshirt in case it's cooler by the lake.

> Me: I always thought going out with you meant you would be talking me out of my clothes not trying to get me to wear more.

> ThatPizzaKy: I don't get naked on the first date.

Me: I think that you are lying to me.

> ThatPizzaKy: *Smiley face* Okay. I don't want to get naked with you on our first date. We have a lot of time ahead of us for moving forward. We don't have to do it all on the first date.

Me: I don't know if I should feel special or offended.

> ThatPizzaKy: I'll be there at 9. Get some sleep. I plan to make you take all the trails on Barter Point tomorrow.

nineteen

· · ·

WE WERE JUST PULLING into the lot at Lake Myron when I started laughing.

"Did you choose this to get me alone in the woods, 'cause that sounds shady." I smiled at him.

He grinned and pulled the car into a spot away from all the others. "To be honest, I'm really happy to have you alone, and also to not be exhausted from a seven hour shift when we are hanging out."

"It was sneaky of you," I said. "Taking my shift tonight, so I didn't have to work after our date. But I need the money, you knucklehead."

"I didn't want you to have a fifteen hour day," he said to me and shrugged. "I will switch you a day since you are getting your car next week. Though I am sad to hear you won't need rides to work anymore. But now, you can pick me up."

We got out and walked to the information map.

Lake Myron was part of the State Park. It had boating, fishing, swimming, picnicking and trails. I hadn't been here since fifth grade when we took a field trip during the summer's Bug Camp. It hadn't changed much. The area we were in was a dirt lot with a map behind plexiglass at the entrance of the trails.

As for the trails themselves? There were all sorts: long and short hikes, scenic and even ones with sharp inclines. Despite his threat to make me do all the trails, we studied the map that indicated the most scenic would be three miles long, from trailhead to end. It stayed along the lakeside much of the way and was flatter than most, and since I had not followed directions and wore Keds without socks, we needed to stay somewhere intermediate.

We picked up some hoagies and bottles of water prior and packed them in Ky's backpack, along with the first aid kit he insisted we bring.

"So you know what's nice about today?" Ky grinned and took my hand as we walked into the woods.

"It's sunny and the temperature is nice, I'm here with you, and if I play my cards right, I might get a goodnight kiss out of this," I jokingly listed off.

"Well, besides all of that." He swung our arms back and forth happily as we held hands.

I looked out at the water as the path led directly there. "That you're all mine today?" I smiled, avoiding his gaze. I was rather embarrassed at how bold I had gotten.

"Am I?" He was quiet, "I'd like to be. Would you be mine?"

I turned. "What exactly are you asking?"

He looked down then out at the water before peeking back at me through his eyelashes. "I'm not good at this. I just don't want to belong to anyone else. So maybe I should be happy just being yours and have it be okay with that."

I must have taken too long to reply because he turned and started walking along the path pulling me with him.

"I'm going to miss our midnight excursions when we start working different shifts. I don't think Ricky realized we'd become..." He shrugged at his loss for words.

"Co-dependent?" I joked.

"Attached at the hip," he clarified.

"I'm going to miss you too. We will have to text one another in all our extra time like regular couples do." I swallowed after saying that to his back. Apparently, I had a lot of courage when I wasn't looking in his eyes.

He pulled to a stop and turned around though. He looked at me and grinned. "Do you mean that?"

"That I'm a stage five clinger?" I nodded.

He leaned toward me, and I looked into his gray eyes. "Are you going to kiss me?" he whispered.

"I thought you didn't do that until the end of the first date," I whispered back, feeling breathless with anticipation.

He let my hand drop and moved away from me as his lips twitched. He turned and started walking on a part of the trail that narrowed, and I couldn't get ahead of him to stop him.

I grunted. He was teasing me, and I was really about done waiting to be kissed. "Can we negotiate?" I asked trailing after him.

"Is this a hostage situation?" he asked over his shoulder with his eyebrow raised, before he continued walking.

"It might be. Will your parents miss you?" I grabbed a fist full of his shirt and pulled him to a stop. "Don't go any further, Linley!"

"I assured my mother that I would be home at a decent hour since you weren't working tonight, and I have tests in the morning. By the way, she likes Sophie's hair." He tried to take another step, but I grabbed his arm.

"Don't try to change the subject. Okay... I want a logic test here. If you chose the location, don't you think I should choose the activity?" I asked petulantly.

"I don't know if dating is a democracy." He smirked, then pulled me to him. "You want a hug?"

I growled.

"I'm not one of those guys you can take out and tempt me to do bad things. I've learned it pays to be a gentleman." He pulled me into a hug.

"You were my first kiss," I confessed.

"You were the only girl that ever mattered," he whispered in my ear. Then, he laughed. "I don't want you to compromise our reputations."

I slapped his stomach and pushed him away. "Compromise our reputations. You suck."

He pulled me back and laughed, and I went. "I like you too much to mess it up. I'm scared you are going to run away."

"Well, your reputation assures me that you have no qualms about compromising reputations. You kiss without reservation. Stop making me wait!" I grumbled with a pout.

He tilted my head back, and his eyes skimmed over my face. "You're beautiful, Jacelyn. But... you shouldn't listen to gossip! I'm not saying I won't kiss you, just to make you wait. It has to be perfect. Good things come to those who wait."

I narrowed my eyes at him. I dropped my arms from around his waist, pulling away and walked ahead of him "This better be the best kiss you ever gave, Linley. You have built it up now," I said loud enough for him to hear me as he stood where I left him.

His reply was a chuckle that led to an all out laugh that echoed across the lake. "Why can't I find a nice girl who will like me for me!?" He ran up behind me, grabbed me and started to tickle me. "I adore you, Jacelyn."

His words were like a zap to my stomach that awakened the butterflies and caused them to flutter in their confused state. Was *adoration* like *love*?

We walked in silence for a while, then we started talking about everything and anything. His favorite food was macaroni and cheese. He loved his grandmother, but his grandfather was a jackass. We had a lot to laugh about, and it all felt so effortless. Time passed so quickly.

"There is a flat rock ahead that looks over the lake. Let's stop there and have our sandwiches." Ky grabbed my hand and tugged me along. The rock was raised, so I had to climb a bit to get on it. Once on top, there was a really beautiful view over the point. I sat with my legs dangling off the edge and watched a boat that was really far away as it moved through the water. The wake caused the water on the edge of the lake to smack the rocks.

"Have you been out there on one of the boats?" He nodded toward the lake.

"Never. The only people I know with a boat are Alex and Trick, and I'd rather be in the water than on a boat with Trick," I said flatly, to which he grinned.

Ky nudged my shoulder causing me to look up at him as he sat next to me. "Want to go out with me on Friday?"

"On a boat?" My brows twitched.

"We have one down on the lake house on Ballant," he said.

"You have another house?" I said, tilting my head.

He laughed. "We don't live in it. It's an investment. We rent it to vacationers. We dock the boat there in the summer so that we can use it if we want."

"Not to be rude, but I've known you all my life... Why

didn't I know you had money? And why are you living like me, if you do, and working five days a week if you don't need to?" I watched his face curiously.

Ky shrugged dismissively. "We don't need to flash it around for people to see. My parents taught us from when we were young that money isn't what we should impress people with. I was obnoxious about it the year you were ignoring me. I flashed expensive shit around and tried to buy friends. The fact remains that my parents worked really hard for what we have. My dad still works hard, and my mom's healthcare is expensive. We don't need to announce to the world that we have more of anything than anyone else does—it's no one's business.

"And my dad works hard, so why shouldn't I? I do need to cover my school bills. I let my parents use some of my college fund to cover some of mom's medical care. Chemo and radiation is expensive. Wildly so. We don't need anyone to think we are entitled to anything just because we have money. I don't want people to think I should go somewhere more than a state school, or Sophie should be a fashionista."

"Your sister said that your family is very private. I just find it weird that I watched you for years, yet never noticed." I swallowed before I could say anything dumb. I didn't know how to explain my obsession with him, to him.

"Just how long did you study me?" he whispered.

I felt my face flame, and I tried to turn away, but he caught my chin pulling my face up to meet his eyes. "You know you are breathtaking when you do that?"

I rolled my eyes and bit my lip. "I'm breathtaking when my speckled face turns pink? I think more boys would have told me that if it were true," I said wryly.

He shook his head. "I've always thought your freckles were beautiful. I want to count them."

I giggled. "I don't think numbers go that high. And don't use the B-word so freely. I know what I look like and your blatant flattery, without a kiss backing it up, is giving mixed signals."

He smiled. "B-word? Is beautiful a bad word now? Will I have to come clean during confession all the times I tell you that you are beautiful?" His thumb came up to my face and softly caressed my cheek.

"Okay, you know how I said that if you turned out to be a monster there wouldn't be any more dates? It's along the same lines if you feed me bullshit." I shook my head. It felt too much like a rom-com moment.

He shook his head and chuckled sadly. "I can't win, can I? I can't ever tell you how I feel, it's always going to feel like a line. It's because of how we started and that, 'You're so sexy' line when I was in tenth grade. I have to tell you, I've been an ass, but I've never lied to you."

I hated the way I felt right then. I was so uncomfortable with the seriousness of the conversation. It was my mom's fault. She responded to seriousness with jokes. It was my dad's fault he responded to seriousness by ignoring it. And that's why I didn't know how to respond to an actual serious conversation because I'd never seen them through. I'd only seen confrontation and those made sense, and I could get angry and let Ky have it right now, but that was wholly unwarranted.

I shook my head, frustrated with myself. "I'm going to push you in the lake. Enough talk, let's get back on the trail." I moved to stand, when he grabbed my hand and turned me around.

"Wait! No! Sit with me a little longer. I just want to talk

to you for a bit more. I swear no more flowery words. Just plain old talk." The look in his eyes was imploring. He wanted to spend more time talking to me. When I sat back down, he didn't let go of my hand, his fingers lightly stroking and playing along mine.

He cleared his throat and looked out at the water. "Actually, one more serious thing. I know I've been uncomfortable around you sometimes. Awkward even. I don't want you to think it's you. I want to be sure I do it right this time. I want a real foundation, friends first. I think we've been doing that. You've become a really good friend of mine. The other day, it struck me that the butterflies haven't been as bad lately." His gray eyes looked at me and held mine. "This..." He pointed from me to him. "...matters to me."

I smiled. "I know. I feel the same way. I really love spending time with you."

He grinned and turned more my way. I stood, looking down over him as he grinned. "It's part of my ploy."

"You have a ploy?" I raised my brows.

He grabbed my wrist and pulled me into him. I found myself sitting on a boy's lap for the first time in my life. There was a moment where I was stiff until his arms came around me, and his nose nuzzled my hair. "I do have a ploy! Remember? You and I are on our first date. After I take you home, I have to go buy you an engagement ring. Then we get married, in a few years, after college, we will make your mom very happy and give her grandbabies."

"WOAH, slow your roll!" I laughed. "Ky, my mom wanted you to get a fake ID and get me drunk, so I wouldn't be so responsible. Nowhere in our conversation was there talk of marriage and babies. That should be a given. Boys don't talk about that stuff until they are thirty these days. Jump on the train.

"You've misinterpreted my mom's hopes for me. She wants me to be a teenager, not so much of an adult."

Ky's lips brushed against my neck as he smiled. "I see... so should we do something devilish and make her eyebrows raise."

I leaned back and raised mine, and he grinned at me. "Whatever are you thinking, Ky Linley?"

"When do you turn eighteen?" He grinned.

"Is this something I need to be eighteen for?" I hummed. "That is a responsible thing. We need to do it before then."

"Possibly." He nodded.

"I will be eighteen in August though." I leaned against him, relaxing more in his embrace and settling into his lap.

I didn't think Ky was aware that his thumb was rubbing against my arm as he was thinking things through.

"What devilishness are you thinking of?" I leaned closer hoping I might be able to steal a kiss.

"How open are you to piercings? Tattoos?" He laughed. "They are extreme and should make her very proud."

"I would have to put a lot of thought into a tattoo. Piercings on the other hand are something I have already thought about, and there are a few I want to get."

It was Ky's turn to arch his brow, and the most provocative smile I had ever seen touched his lips. Like a moth lured to a flame, I leaned down toward his smile, but he pulled away and wagged his finger between us. "Jacelyn Waverly! Don't try to kiss me in a moment of weakness!"

I whimpered at my plan being foiled. He smirked and asked, "When do you want to go get a piercing, so we can impress your mom with your act of childish rebellion?"

"Soon!" I grinned. "There's a place in town called St. Mark's Piercing. My mom knows the owner."

"Mark Delano? My dad went to school with him. I see a plan forming." Ky laughed. "It will have to be after graduation. What do you want to get pierced?"

"None of your business, boyfriend," I said playfully. I pointed to the trail and its marker, nodding my chin in the direction. "We should go though. We have another mile according to that marker."

I made him walk in front of me, so I could unashamedly check out his backside. I was no longer feeling embarrassed about liking him. He joked about our future marriage. He clearly was comfortable with me too.

Ky started to tell me about why he didn't want to play college football. I had never thought about what a jock did when they left high school. I always thought jocks obviously continued on, but Ky wasn't, and not all people had the opportunity.

"Where will most of the players be in a year or two? What happens to the guys who play in high school that don't go anywhere?" I stumbled on a root, and he caught me before I landed on my face.

Once I straightened, he checked me over and shook his head at my Keds. "You need real shoes next time we do this." He hugged me again before letting me go and shrugged. "I guess they become trainers, business majors, or they take mathematics classes, literature maybe... definitely fail psych class. They can do anything, Jace. It's not like there is a home for high school football stars. You don't get shoveled off into zombieland. Although, some might disappear into obscurity and work at Piero's or some other minimum wage job."

I shrugged. "So many of them are dumb."

"See? That's a stereotype. We don't just use our heads to bash into one another. We have to maintain a GPA to play sports. You can't just have other people do your home-work. You have to take tests, exams and do projects. If you can't hack it, you have to get a tutor that can help bring you up to speed, but you can't just be stupid and get by. Did you think I was dumb because I played sports?" he asked, sounding frustrated.

I pursed my lips and decided to take the joking way out. "Well, you do let other guys hit you on the field in the fall, and balls come at your head in the spring."

He turned around and gave me a look. "I'm not a boxer, you know. I don't stand and just let them clip me on the jaw. I've never been hurt in a game. I find your view of sports players insulting."

I lifted a shoulder. "Maybe if you kissed me, it would change my mind."

He laughed. "You really want a kiss that badly? You've done it before. It's not like you haven't already experienced the act."

"It was a long time ago. I've forgotten if it was good or not. I need to compare it to Javi," I joked. But it was a lie. I remember every second of my first kiss with Ky Linley.

"Javi, huh? Forgettable boything Javi?" Ky smiled knowingly.

"One and the same." I nodded. "He kissed me without having me beg."

"If I kiss you, will you be happy?" he whispered, step-ping closer to me.

I gave him a huge smile and nodded my head in an over-exaggerated affirmation. I stood waiting.

"Close your eyes, Jacelyn," he whispered, framing my jaw in his palm.

I closed them, and tilted my head up to his. I felt his breath on my face then felt a light kiss on the tip of my nose. I opened my eyes and looked at him. "Ky," I whined. I'd waited for what seemed like forever for his lips on mine, and instead got little more than a cuddle kiss.

"You didn't specify what kind of kiss. You have to admit I did kiss you, and you said you'd be happy. So stop looking at me like that." He grinned.

I stepped back and touched my nose. "You know when you finally kiss me, I'm going to make you regret all your teasing."

"I hope so," he said, grabbing my hand and leading me down the path.

twenty

· · ·

IT WAS BARELY NOON when we finished the trail. We talked about taking another, but were both getting hungry again, and I needed to go to the bathroom. We hopped in the car and drove to the nearest park restrooms, I was able to use them without gagging and wash the sweat from my face. I went back out to the car. "What are we doing next? We have a few hours before our day has to end."

Ky looked at me. "Don't you want to go home and have your kiss?"

I laughed. "Well, yeah. But I also like spending time with you. I like spending time with you a lot. I want to spend a lot of time with you."

He smiled in response to the look on my face and started the car. "Let's go to my house."

I grabbed his arm. "Does that mean the date is over?"

He shook his head. "No, we are still on the date."

I sighed, looked out the window and whispered under my breath, "Booooo!"

When we arrived at his house, no one was home.

He tossed his keys on the foyer table and led me into the

kitchen and started making me a cheese, lettuce and tomato sandwich. "Do you want to watch TV downstairs or up in my room?"

I felt confident he wouldn't suddenly get handsy, especially considering how difficult he was being with giving me a simple kiss. "Upstairs. What are we going to watch?"

"Up to you," he said as he made our sandwiches.

He placed them on plates and carried them upstairs. "I forgot the drinks. Make yourself comfortable and find something to watch while I go grab us something to drink." He set down the plate onto his bed before jogging down the steps.

I flipped through the channels before settling on SpongeBob SquarePants and made myself comfy on his bed. He had some throw pillows on his bed like others often did, so I grabbed one to set it on my lap while I took a huge bite of my sandwich. I watched him reenter his room with fruit roll-ups and an entire pack of grape flavored juice boxes.

"What the hell? Are you serious? You are my dream man!" I laughed.

"I know the way to a girl's heart is with sugar." He dropped the items on the foot of the bed and kicked off his shoes before dropping down next to me. He looked at the screen as he reached for a fruit roll up. "I see you chose a classic."

We watched two episodes and when the third came on, I turned to him. I couldn't help myself, I stared at his profile and smiled until he looked my way. We were less than a foot apart and had been sitting shoulder to shoulder before I had moved to face him. Our fingers were intertwined and rested on his thigh. I was happy, truly, sincerely happy.

Before I realized what I was doing, I leaned over and

softly pressed my lips to his with courage I hadn't known I had in me. Though to be fair, it was a kickass kiss. When I pulled away, I licked my lips and tasted cherry fruit roll-up.

"Waiting, is something you are very terrible at," he whispered after a bit. "And you are bad at kissing too."

I sat back as my jaw dropped and playfully slapped his arm. "You're such a jackass!"

He laughed and tried to shield himself from my slap. "You told me you were going to make me regret not kissing you when we finally did. That did nothing in the way of rocking my world on any level," he teased and pouted in mock disappointment.

That was definitely a challenge if I ever heard one.

I sat up onto my heels and started tickling him until he was rolling and kicking around the bed. I had him squealing, snorting and laughing uncontrollably. In turn, I was cackling like a fiend, until he executed his defense attack. He reached up and pulled me down by my nape and rolled over to pin me down before he kissed me.

It wasn't a quick peck on the lips or anything too light. It was a real, deep kiss!

I was swept away with the sudden rearrangement of our bodies, then on the wave of butterflies along with something else I couldn't determine, as his other hand traveled from the side of my body up to play with my hair. His legs became tangled with mine, confusing me where I started and he ended; we were lost in one another.

For a moment during our makeout session, I was distracted when SpongeBob and Squidward fought over something, but Ky whispered, "I'll turn it off if you can't multitask, Jace!" which made me laugh while he kissed me silly.

Things honestly got out of hand, until we laid next to

one another on his bed, both of us breathing heavily. He looked over at me with swollen lips and fixed my shirt, which had gotten out of place. "Fuck me," he breathed out. "I should say I'm sorry because that went from one-to-sixty in about thirty seconds, but I'm not sorry. Making out with you is fun."

"Well, we only really went to second base, can you imagine if we went further?" I giggled and bit my lip.

Ky licked his lips. "No, I don't think I'm quite ready for more than that."

"Does this mean our date is over?" My voice sounded foreign to me. It was breathy and a little weak. "Am I still a bad kisser?"

It was his turn to laugh. "Ongoing research over time will determine that."

I grabbed the throw pillow next to me and playfully hit him with it. He was quick though and grabbed my wrist to halt my attack and pulled me back his way, pressing his lips to mine lightly before saying, "We might need to stick with one another until you're expert level, I'll help you study. But I really want to officially upgrade from friends to a more exclusive situation soon. You can't just use me for my body."

I gazed at him and took in the brightness of his gray eyes and the rosiness of his cheeks after our kissing. He was definitely the beautiful one in this relationship. "Are you saying that you want me to be your study buddy?" The corner of my lips quirked upward as I teased.

Ky shook his head. His finger came up and started lightly skimming my cheekbone. I smiled when I saw his lips move and silently mouth numbers; he was counting my freckles. His eyes climbed up towards my temple and his lips briefly met mine before he shook his head. "No. Not a study buddy. I want you to just be mine."

"Don't our parents already think I'm yours and that you're mine?" I looked from one gray eye to the other and noticed that one had more blue in it than the other.

"What our parents think, and what you think, don't appear to be the same thing." His lips ran along my jaw.

"And you are running a campaign at the moment to change that?" I asked, coyly.

"This?" He kissed my mouth again, and we got lost in the moment for a bit. When he pulled away, he chuckled. "No, this is me getting to live out a fantasy I know you want just as much as I do. The exclusive thing is separate. Don't make me beg like a simp. Will you please be my girl?"

He was one to talk, considering I had begged for him to kiss me and finally took matters into my own hands. Despite that, I was willing to give him an answer but before I could, the front door opened and closed, interrupting any room for conversation or fantasizing.

Ky rolled off of the bed, adjusted himself, cleared his throat and headed to his ensuite. "Can you do something about the bed?" He stopped at the bathroom door and turned. "I should clarify it was definitely worth the wait. I don't remember you kissing like that the first time. I hate Javi if he was the one to teach you that."

I couldn't help laughing as I straightened the bed, throw pillows included. "I practiced with my pillow at night."

"What a lucky pillow," he sighed longingly, before closing the door behind him.

A few minutes later, there was a knock at his bedroom door before it opened. Sandra stood there and smiled on the other side of the doorway. "I didn't realize you were here! Are you hungry? I'm thinking of getting Carter to pick something up for dinner."

She didn't look concerned that I was on Ky's bed or the

fact I had been alone with him in his room. If anything, she was happy I was here. Maybe she was like my mom. *Oh God, we didn't need two of them!*

"I am hungry," I admitted, as Ky came out of the bathroom. I looked over at him and realized he looked like we had been making out. Then I realized I probably looked like that too. Oh, Heavens! His mom wasn't t dumb, she knew!

Carter ended up bringing home Chinese from a place in Maystown that Sandra loved. Ky spent ten minutes telling his mom all about our morning while she nodded and asked questions. Carter was more reserved as he had his iPad open, and was looking at some housing specs.

"Oh, by the way, I need you to go in late on Wednesday. Sophie has to go to Dr. Aaron after school," Sandra said, pointing her chopsticks Ky's way.

Ky tensed, and I suddenly felt like I had overheard something I wasn't supposed to. "We can talk about it later," he replied.

Sandra looked from him to me and back, a flicker of disapproval crossed her face. I wasn't sure if it was towards Ky or me.

She sighed and started another topic, this one towards me. "I heard you finished a year early and graduated a few months before Maris and Ky. Did you like homeschooling?"

"To an extent. It was more about convenience since San Diego, and to a larger extent California, education is vastly different than here. I wanted to go to public school, but it was in some ways very far ahead, and in other ways behind where I already was. I found that in some cases, I was going to have to retake some freshman classes, while other classes that I'd be signing up for in San Diego would be senior level classes here.

"But when I hear Maris, Peter and Sophie talking about

social things happening at school, I feel like I missed out on a lot of things."

Ky smirked sympathetically. "Peter and Soph are turning into a two person cliqué. I think you would want to come back just to play your people watching games with those two. They are trouble with a capital T–right now by giving Gaven hell."

"Carter Kyrin Linley you are one to talk! You were a handful with your friends for a good while before you straightened up. At least I know that the only thing those two will get into are unique haircuts, nail salons, and boy bashing." Ky's mom chuckled.

It was my turn to smirk. I knew that Ky had kept his debauchery from his mom, so I figured I could ask about his haymaking days. "What was Ky doing that got him and his friends in trouble?"

Ky cringed, shook his head, and gave a dramatic whimpering plea. "Let's not go into this."

Sandra shook her head as if telling Ky he wasn't off the hook. "I got a call midway through Ky's ninth grade year about how he and his friends were truants. I called the mothers of all his posse, and they were just as clueless as to where the boys might have been. I went to the most logical place that he might be." She paused for dramatic effect.

I smiled and filled in the blank. "Piero's?"

She nodded. "Piero's. There were six of them, and they had been smoking on the side of the building, but Ricky let them in, gave them pizza, and wouldn't let them leave without putting them to work cleaning the bathrooms."

I laughed as I imagined Ricky making Ky clean toilets.

"He told me the next time I was caught skipping school, he'd give me a job cleaning urinals by hand. Vile shit."

"But you didn't skip without letting us know after that."

Carter smiled. "And it got you an in with Ricky when you wanted a job."

"That's enough of that, I think." Ky took a bite of his beef and broccoli.

I disagreed though. "I don't think so. Gimme more."

Ky pouted at me, and Sandra smiled. She thought quietly then nodded. "When Ky was in his sophomore year, he was an arrogant brat. He was growing into all his limbs and football was filling out the rest, he was good looking and girls were noticing him. He knew himself to be a catch, and it was his weakness."

I looked over at him to find he had his head down and looked both sad and sickened by the story his mom was telling. His shoulder slumped when she continued.

"He had just got his new cell phone, one that we didn't monitor daily. I had lectured him again and again about appropriate phone etiquette and behavior. He had it about two months when Carter became curious. He didn't want to necessarily snoop, but he wanted to know if Ky was doing anything he shouldn't be doing." She sighed.

"He looked at my text history and went ballistic," Ky whispered, he dropped his head in his hand. "Jace knows how this ends."

"No, I don't," I said quietly.

"Well, Carter had a talk with him. Ky gave a ton of atti-tude, and we threatened to take the damn thing away if he didn't use it appropriately. He gave so much lip service about how 'everyone did it.' Then one day he came home and handed us the phone and said he didn't want it. We thought he was joking, so we kept waiting for him to ask for it back. In the meantime, did I ever get an education in the joys of teenage boy texting? Apparently, he was right...

Everyone he was talking to seemed to be doing what he was doing. It was an epidemic."

I looked over at Ky whose entire body had deflated. It was like all the happiness we had shared today had been drained out.

"Not everyone." He shook his head.

"Finally one day, I cornered him before he left for school and demanded he tell me why he suddenly went lo-tech." She looked at me as I gave her my full attention. She knew she was imparting something life changing. "Ky confessed that his cellphone helped him act like an asshole. He said when he was an asshole, he ruined things and that he ruined the only thing he had truly wanted when he finally had it."

I looked at him and felt my lower lip tremble. He stood and came to me, wrapping his arms around me. "I'm so sorry, Jacelyn. I never meant to hurt you."

I heard Sandra stand and drag her husband out of the room to give us privacy.

Ky continued, "I was young and dumb and so stupid."

"I knew, Ky," I said tearfully. His fingers came up to wipe the runaway tears from my cheeks, and I grabbed his hand. "I always knew." I looked into his worried face. I could see the concern in his eyes. I couldn't just sense his regret, I could see the pervasive sadness he wore in his heart over what had happened so long ago.

"What did you know?" he whispered.

I shook my head and leaned up to kiss his lips. "I always knew that you weren't callous and mean at heart. I knew you wouldn't purposefully hurt me. I knew that the things you said that day weren't a reflection of your heart." I wrapped my arms around his shoulder and wiggled the one trapped against his chest out to hug him against me.

He grabbed my arms and pushed me away from him. "Jace, I did do those things though. I didn't realize the consequences. I never meant for them to hurt you. I just wasn't thinking with anything but my ego and my..." he looked down but didn't say it. I knew what he meant though.

"I don't want to keep thinking about it. I don't want to hold onto the past. We are older now," I said. "It was years ago. Maris keeps it recent enough without us rehashing it. I've forgiven you. I forgave you a while ago. Please stop beating yourself up about it and just treat me right now, going forward. You and me? Right?"

He nodded and quickly brushed his lips against mine. "Yeah, you and me are in this together emotionally, but I want to do this right though, physically. Don't you want me to treat you with respect and show you how I feel?"

I looked into his eyes. " Are you not into me right now?"

He squeezed his eyes shut and inhaled through his nose. "This is like walking through a landmine... I feel like I just stepped very close to danger." He took a moment to measure his words carefully. "I want you. I have always wanted you. That's why I want to wait for all the good things with you, so it will mean more to us. Just touching you today showed me I can easily lose my head, and my hormones can make me act rashly. I forgot all about how I wanted to go slow while I was kissing you. But I don't want our first time to be on my bed while SpongeBob plays, and my mom can walk in at any moment. It's got to be perfect, or damn near as special as possible."

"Are you going to make me wait until we are married before we have sex?" I ask him in disbelief.

"We just kissed today." He kissed me again. "And when you think of our first time... five, ten, twenty years from now–I want you to think of it and know you were loved more than anything. That it meant everything in the world to me to share the experience with you. There's no possible way I can give you my first kiss or my first time. I'm sorry. I wish I could. But I can make your first time count for something more than just a hormonal fix."

We stared at one another. Then slowly we started laughing. Ky ran his hand through his hair. "Shit. Do I sound like a Hallmark card?" He sighed.

I looked down then poked him in the side. "So you love and cherish me?"

Ky turned pink. "Not quite yet, but it can't be long now."

twenty-one

. . .

ON GRADUATION DAY, my dad called me at nine a.m, which was fine since graduation wasn't until seven at night.

"She still won't talk to me?" my dad asked over the phone.

"No one here, other than me, wants to talk to you," I clarified.

My dad made a sound that seemed distressed. "Jacelyn, I'm in Maystown. I came for Maris' graduation. I got her a present."

"Dad! No! Why?" I closed my eyes and nearly whined.

"She's not just your mother's daughter, she's mine too!" he said, petulantly.

I shook my head even though he couldn't see me. "Maybe you should have considered us before cheating on mom!"

"That's not fair, honey!" He sighed. "Life isn't that simple."

"Dad, life isn't that hard," I retorted before hanging up on him.

I sighed and looked outside at my Beetle. Other than using it for work, I'd been bumming rides off my boyfriend to leave the car to Maris. I figured I owed her something, and she was definitely more laid back since she had some freedom. My mom had apparently been working her over on the Ky point, and the other day she had a conversation with me about him, where she didn't insult him at all.

My head made a clapping sound on the table when I set it down in frustration. My sister came and wrapped her arms around me. "I didn't know you had it in you to fight with our sire."

"I've always talked to him like that. Just because I went with him, didn't mean I agreed with him." I shook my head. "He is here, in town, for your graduation. Apparently, he has something for you." I deadpanned.

"Delusional bastard." She stood and went to get some coffee. "At least he doesn't have a ticket."

I nodded in agreement.

Sandra and Carter had invited me, my mom and Peter to sit with them tonight. Maris got four tickets, and her last one, she wanted to use in her memory book.

"What are you doing today?" I asked her.

"Alex has family stuff, so I've got nothing to do. I'm going to hang out here." She plucked a grape tomato out of the bowl I had on the counter. "Could you teach me to make an omelet?"

I smiled. "Yeah, do you want to watch Bridergerton after that?"

"And talk about boyfriends?" She smiled softly. "I hear you have a steady one now."

I swallowed. "Mare?"

"I'm sorry, Jacelyn. Alex and I had a long talk over the last week, and he confessed to me that he's not friends with people because of me. He's lost friends over being with me. It makes me feel like a shitty girlfriend, so I had a long talk with mom because I don't want to be a shitty sister too," she confessed, looking a little scared.

I stood up a little too fast causing the chair to almost tip over. Suddenly I was in Maris' arms and sobbed uncontrollably. "I needed you to approve so much. I love you so much. Please don't change your mind back to hating Ky."

"He's going to piss me off, Jace, but I will totally give him a chance and not shut him down. I would hate it if you did that to Alex. And I hate that I made Alex do that to people he cared about. I'm a really terrible person." She sniffled.

"You're a hard person, Mare. You expect a lot from people, but not more than you are willing to give." I hugged her again, before moving to start showing her how to make her own omelets.

"I did something unforgivable though," she confessed. "In the heat of it all, I changed our rooming assignments, so we won't be dormed together like we originally talked about. I'm sorry, Jace. I asked for a reassignment, but they can't change it."

I smiled at her. "It's okay. It'll be good for us to get out on our own, we'll still see each other after all."

She sniffled. "I don't want you to think that any of it means I don't want to be your sister."

"I know." I laughed and hugged her. "I'm an awesome little sister."

We watched Bridgerton where my sister went on and on about costuming until I stopped her with a realization. "I think you should major in costume design."

"I don't know a thing about art, nor do I know anyone

who does." She shrugged, while scrunching up her face in distaste. "But it does sound awesome."

"Do Gen Eds for the first two years then transfer to art school." I hit pause on the show before going to get my laptop.

"What are you doing?" She asked as she watched me.

"Seeing if you even need Gen Eds for art school. Maybe save money, take a gap year, then start Art School next year." I typed quickly.

"Are you serious?" She sat watching me.

"What else do you feel passionate about?" I asked her.

She shook her head. "Nothing. What is your passion?"

I laughed. "Education and counseling."

"Go figure." She leaned forward and hugged me.

That night Maris, Mom, Peter and I went out for a family dinner. She didn't even complain about Alex not being there. We went to Sampson's, which unfortunately served a lot of meat, leaving me no other option of food other than a salad, but I didn't want to make a fuss. It wasn't my night.

"Are you excited to walk on stage and get your diploma? Should I say break a leg?" Peter tapped his fork onto his plate, waiting for Mare's answer.

"Please don't say' break a leg.' I'm terrified I'm going to trip and eat shit." She closed her eyes and shook her head as if she could erase the thought from her mind.

"We should finish up soon," my mom stated as she wiped her mouth with a napkin. "We'll get boxes for all the leftovers. Mare has to get to Alex's to get ready. Ignore his mother. Just have fun."

Mom was referring to how Alex's mom was giving Mare and Alex a hard time about them walking together in the procession. She thought they would regret it later on.

Ky nervously approached me the other day about his options. He said he was thinking of walking with Shea, but only because she was the only 'friend' he'd had after things went to hell. It bothered me knowing what she wanted from him, but it was also his graduation, and he needed the high school closure his way.

Mare stood. "Do you want me to take the Bug or your car, mom?"

"We are not all stuffing ourselves in that Beetle. You take the Bug. We are going to be meeting up with the Linleys." My mom waved over the waitresses and asked for take-away boxes and a bag.

My sister scooted out of her seat to hug me. "I love you, thanks for letting me take your car."

I sniffled. "*Mi carro es su carro.*"

"I took French, not Spanish, little sister." We both started laughing. "And I don't even know how I passed that class. All I really know is *fermez la bouche*!"

Peter snorted now. "I would like to tell you to shut your mouth sometimes too."

"Shut up, Peter!" She playfully pushed him and grinned.

My sister was just happier having had a heart to heart with Alex, mom and I. She left on a light note, and I fell into the booth and deflated.

"Dad's here," I groaned.

My mom nodded. "I know. I spoke to Ron. I got him a ticket to graduation."

Peter gasped dramatically, and I gave her a pained look. "No, mom. No! No! No! Maris just sorted herself out!"

"It will be fine. She needs to confront this." She nodded.

"Mom!" I sighed and shook my head, sadly.

"He and I need closure too," my mom admitted.

"I'm so glad I didn't have a big day," I murmured. Peter rubbed my back sympathetically.

We left the restaurant and drove to the school. The Linleys were already there and were set up tailgate style which made me laugh. Sandra, Sophie, Taylor and Carter were relaxing in chairs when we approached. "Sandra. This is going to be a problem for parking." I joked.

"We are so early. We brought graduation party gifts for everyone." She held up a bag filled with little graduation caps and I laughed. She handed me my bag and I opened it, and found it to be like a fortune cookie with a slip of paper peeking out from it.

I slipped the paper out from the graduation cap and read it to myself as Sophie leaned over my shoulder. She started giggling. "Jace's says, '*Don't waste your time on the past, your future is all that matters.*'"

I smiled and held the paper to my heart. Arms wrapped around me from behind, before a kiss was pressed to my cheek. I turned my head even though I knew who had attacked me with affection, "You better be my boyfriend, if you are taking liberties like that."

"I better be the only one who takes liberties." Ky kissed my shoulder and moved, so I could turn to see him.

He was dressed up in a suit, and he looked incredibly handsome. It was then that I understood what the term swoon meant. I covered my mouth, to keep my jaw from dropping, but it didn't work. "You look so good!"

"So you're saying I should dress like this seven days a week? Ricky would love it." He chuckled and looked down at himself.

"He is coming tonight, you know," I told him.

He nodded. "I know. He thinks he single handedly got me through high school and turned me into an upstanding citizen."

I sucked on my lips and felt my face flush when Ky leaned down to kiss me in front of everyone. I looked down shyly, and he laughed. "Get used to it, Jacelyn. We're a thing now."

We hung around until more people started to show, then the Linleys put their chairs away, and we all moved down to the football field where the ceremony was going to take place. We showed our tickets to the lower class person at the booth and had them stamped on the back. Ky kissed me at the ticket booth and left to go back to the school. Sophie linked her arm through mine. "Someday, you, Peter and I will be sisters."

I rolled my eyes and smiled.

My mom and Sandra hit it off and got into a deep discussion about historical Fellsdale. Apparently, my mom and Sandra grew up in the same town a few years apart. They shared a passion for the history of the buildings that had been torn down for industrialization. I heard my mom say, "I hope they never destroy the Catholic Church!"

Sandra nodded in agreement. "My confirmation was there!"

"I was married there," my mom added.

Taylor slid next to me and grinned. He had his Nintendo Switch in his hands for a moment, then grabbed his backpack and pulled the case out to put it away. "Do you have your phone, Jace?" he asked me.

I gave him a teasing look. "You have yours don't you, do you need two?"

An amused chuckle that was alarmingly similar to Ky's

came from him. Taylor shook his head. "Download Marvel Snap. It's a Ben Brode developed online card game that is tons of fun to play."

"Who is Ben Brode?" I asked.

He opened his mouth to answer and shook his head. "Doesn't matter. Someday, I'll get you up to speed on gaming, and you will understand who everyone is."

I laughed. "Okay." Once I downloaded it and started playing, it took me about ten seconds to know it wasn't anything like solitaire. Taylor was patient, teaching me step by step the basics as we waited for the ceremony to start.

When the procession started, Taylor cleared his throat to catch my attention. I hadn't known how sucked into the game I had gotten until that moment, and I found Taylor grinning at me in a knowing manner. "I want you to know, if my brother ever screws up, there is another option in the Linley family." He blushed, and I felt my cheeks flare red too. Sophie must have been listening because she leaned in. "Well, if you want to experiment, there are two options."

Peter snorted and shook his head. "You're not gay."

"I could be," Sophie said, winking and sitting back.

I leaned into Taylor and replied. "It's good to know I don't have to shop around. I love the Linleys, I'd hate to have to get to know a new family."

He shrugs. "Works out well for both of us then." A moment passed before we started laughing. It earned us a reprimand as several shushes came from surrounding families. When his dad turned around to give the once shy younger sibling a raised eyebrow in question to his antics, Taylor put his arm around me and winked. "Just putting the moves on my brother's girl."

It made us laugh again and in turn, receive tsks and

growls from the surrounding families again. I turned around and gave them my own scowl.

It took forever for the names to be called, then finally they got to the L's. When Ky walked up, we all whopped and celebrated. Some kids had made goofy faces to get laughs as they got their diploma like Shawn Getty who fist bumped Assistant Principal Ritali, rather than shaking his hand, and Megan Andrews kissed his cheek. Eddie Keating had whipped open his gown to reveal his Batman shorts underneath.

I didn't expect any kind of foolery from Ky though.

When he got up there, I noticed I could see bare legs, and when he moved his arms, I couldn't see his suit jacket or dress shirt. He did have on bright pink sneakers though. As he made it to the top of the ramp, he unzipped his gown and dropped it from his shoulders.

I looked to Sandra to see her hand covering her mouth in shock. Sophie was laughing, and Taylor's shoulders were shaking.

"What–?"

Before my question could be formed, he turned and his chest was painted white with a pink ribbon. He turned around and on his back was written in black. 'One fight won. One fight begun!'

I looked at Sophie, her laughter had stopped and tears were running down her face.

The crowd was silent, sensing that this had a deeper meaning than some random tom foolery, until Carter stood and started applauding. Everyone stood and joined in. I was surprised to see Maris was one of the first to join.

My boyfriend was soon ushered off the stage, but despite that, he looked happy. He blew kisses our way and took his seat. I noticed that he had replaced his cap with a pink one that sparkled and had a pink ribbon to match.

When Maris' turn came, she got up and dropped her gown to reveal she was also dressed in pink with white writing that read 'I stand for those who fight.' My mom turned to me, and her eyes were wet. She grabbed me and sobbed. "You're sister always manages to surprise me sometimes."

Alex also wore a pink breast cancer awareness shirt, and smirked when Mr. Ritali announced that the next person who disturbed the ceremony would not receive their diploma tonight which, in turn, received many boos.

The ceremony finished without another 'disturbance' but with a moving speech from the valedictorian. Then, the time came for when the caps were tossed and graduates were let go. The song "I Lived" by OneRepublic started playing as the students left their chairs and moved to their families. My mom saw my dad making a beeline for Maris, but she cut him off to derail the confrontation. Sandra looped her arm through mine.

"It was an incredible ceremony," I said, emotion still clogging my throat.

She sniffled and nodded. "Beautiful. He looks good in pink."

I laughed. "He could have used a little help picking out the body paint color though. The shoes were the right color."

"You might be right, boys are notoriously bad for picking shades of pink." She smiled.

Peter clucked his tongue and came up next to us. "Mrs L. I know you did not just toss me into the pot with the pink potluck pickers."

I felt her hand squeeze my arm reflexively as she

laughed. "Of course not, Peter. You are a superior pink picker. Look at your hair." She touched his pink shock of hair. "You have style. Perhaps you can teach Ky a thing or two."

I looked back to where my mom and dad were, finding them with Mare, who looked sick. I hated that they did this to her. Glancing around, I saw Taylor and Carter trying to get Alex and Ky's attention, who were surrounded by a bunch of people and were busy giving them high fives and congratulations.

Sandra looked around, and I pulled her further out of the path of people. "Let's just wait until everyone comes to us." She started to move back, but I grabbed both her hands to get her attention. I had thought it was weird to treat her like an equal at first instead of an authority figure, but now, I was grabbing her hands like we were buddies. I must've drank too much of the Linley Kool-Aid.

"Is there food after this, Mrs. L? I must admit, I ate well earlier, but this one didn't and sustenance is necessary." Peter pointed at me.

"Peter, stop calling me Mrs. L. Call me Sandra," she insisted, "We can go back to the house and whip something up."

"My dad's here." I sighed with disappointment. "I don't know if we can go. We might have to have a family blow-out. Actually, would you excuse me?"

Sandra hugged me. "Come back before you leave." She made me promise before she let me go.

I wandered over to the three people who looked tense and uncomfortable. "Jacelyn!" My dad greeted me. He knew better than to try to hug me. We had burnt that bridge a long time ago. "I came to give your sister a gift." He held out a key. "I got her a car that matches yours but in her favorite color."

"What did you get mom?" I asked.

My mom gave me a warning look.

I shook my head. "No, mom. He can't do this. He can't come in and out of our lives with presents to make up for being an absentee dad. He is either in a full time position, or he gives it up. And he definitely can't neglect to try to make amends and fail to get you something when he's hurt you the most."

Maris looked at me surprised.

"You need to leave, and take a long look at your life to figure out your priorities. If we are priorities to you, then you need to call us more than once a month and make more of an effort than the extreme gift giving and give fewer excuses. Maris and I are a package. You don't get me without her. If she isn't ready for you, I'm not either."

"Wait." My sister grabbed my hand. "I want to do family counseling with dad. We can do it virtually with him in California... If he's willing..."

My mom looked troubled, misinterpreting what Maris meant. I smiled at her reassuringly. "You're off the hook, she's talking about me and her and him. You've gone through enough, mom."

She took a deep breath and sighed with relief.

My dad looked down though and shook his head. "I'll think about it... We can talk about it later. I'll go now. Your car is parked in slot 245."

Maris' shoulders fell with disappointment, and my mom gave my dad a scathing look as he walked away with his tail between his legs. "He's a shitball," Mare gritted out.

"A big shitball," my mom agreed.

"I thought he'd take the olive branch," I admitted with

disappointment. But on the other hand, I was really proud of Maris for making such a big step. I know it couldn't have been easy.

My mom shook her head and pulled us into her arms. "He's always been a selfish bastard. I'm sorry girls." There was so much love and sense of family in our trio embrace. It gave me hope. Even if dad never made an effort, we still had each other, and we were each incredible in our own way.

"Mare!" Alex came up from behind her and waited until she pulled away from our shared embrace. He spun her around and searched her face. "You okay?"

"I will be." She sighed sadly. Whether she meant it or not, I knew she would be eventually. We would all be okay.

twenty-two

. . .

RICKY PULLED the toothpick he'd been chewing on out of his mouth and shook his head. "So what you want me to do is hire Jace's sister Maris, give her Jace's position, move Jace to the dining room and fire you?"

"What?" My eyes went round with surprise at what I was hearing.

Ky snorted and kicked Ricky's foot. "You couldn't function without me, old man, and we don't know what you are going to do yet come fall when Jace and I leave for college. Mare might be your saving grace."

"She's taking a gap year?" Ricky sighed. "Why? No. Don't tell me. You kids drive me crazy."

"She's also going to be working with the interior designer that works with my dad on consulting. It's just not a lot of hours," Ky explained.

Ricky nodded. "I'll hire her part-time to start. Jacelyn moves to the dining room, which works out, because I just had Angelina in here wanting to change her shift, and I had no one to cover her. Ky, you are going to train Jace. No funny stuff at work. If I find you two kissing in the bathroom again, you're both fired."

Ky smirked. "Goes for you too. Next time I find you making out with Martina back here, I own the business."

"Get the fuck out of here, you little shit," Ricky ordered with a smirk of his own.

Ky took my hand, which made Ricky wad up a piece of paper and throw it at Ky's head. "No fraternizing."

"Not on open hours, but we aren't open yet!" Ky negotiated, pulling me down the hall.

There was a lunch crowd on Monday and it was not busy, the perfect time to learn and not difficult work. I already knew the menu inside and out and could answer as to what ingredients were in menu items. Ky quizzed me as I rattled information from the top of my head and when he was satisfied, he left me alone. Unlike my first day in the kitchen, I wasn't nervous about being a waitress, not even when things got busy. My only handicap was learning to carry out the food tray.

I would have to practice that.

My hours were ten a.m. to six in the evening. I got food to take home and waited for Ky to come back from his last delivery. We were heading back to my house to hang out with Alex, Maris, Peter and Sophie, when a voice startled me.

"Hey, I'm looking for Jacelyn," someone said to the hostess. At the mention of my name, I looked up to find the culprit and saw a good looking guy.

I stood up from the table I was at and moved to him. "I'm Jacelyn. Who are you?"

He swallowed and his Adam's apple bobbed nervously. "I'm Gaven."

My eyebrows raised. "Oh!" I crossed my arms over my

chest and glared at him; I had nothing to say to this guy. Not after what he did to Peter.

"I've been trying to get in touch with Peter. He and Sophie won't talk to me. I–um, I came out to my parents. I want to talk to him. Could you tell him I–"

"I'll tell him you stopped by," I said in a monotone voice.

"Will you tell him, I'm coming–"

"If he asks. I'm not volunteering any information about you that will set him up for more heartache. You were a real shit to him. I don't care what you do in your life. But coming out, can't heal the pain you caused him," I said.

"I heard you were forgiving. That's why I approached you," he said, sounding desperate and whiny.

"So, are you looking for my forgiveness or his?" I narrowed my eyes.

He looked down. "...I'll keep trying."

"Good idea," Ky said, joining us. "I fucked up and no one could fix it, but me. Don't expect intercedence to save you."

Gaven didn't say anything else and left with his shoulders hunched over in a humble manner. I watched him leave. "I don't like him,"

Ky tongued his cheek and laughed. "Okay, Mare Junior. I guess you know where your sister was coming from when she was standing between us ."

My shoulders fell and I shook my head. "Whatever."

We arrived at my house surprised to find Sophie there too. I hadn't seen her in a few days.

She had confided in Peter and I that a lump had been detected in her breast three weeks ago, and it was benign, but she had been terrified. She had a consultation with oncology anyway, with her mom in tow, to discuss the legacy she shared with the women in her family. It was emotional, and she was a mess. She demanded mocktails and hot man movies that night.

Tonight, she looked better.

"Maris!" Ky called, and she came over to hug me.

"We got you a job!" I said excitedly. "With us."

"Ricky's going to let me work there?" She grinned. "Maybe we should get mom a job there too."

I leaned into my sister. "Sandra is setting mom up with a friend of hers. He's wealthy, has a job, and no prior shitty relationship stories on his side."

Mare leaned back and high-fived me. "YES! Tell me he's looking for a babygirl."

I gagged, and Ky laughed.

We all got comfy with the arrangement of Alex and Maris and Sophie and Peter all cuddled up on the couch. Ky and I were seated side by side in the oversized recliner. He kissed me. "Gonna tell Peter about Gaven?"

"Later, when it's just us. I don't want him to feel like he has to perform or react in a specific way to please everyone." I nuzzled his chin.

"You know. You're hard not to fall for Jacelyn." He wrapped an arm around my shoulders and pulled me into him.

"Then stop fighting so hard and submit to your fate. You're mine, Carter Kyrin Linley, now and forever. And there's nothing you can do about it." I smiled before sealing it with a kiss.

epilogue 1

"This is insane. You four are insane," Peter argued.

"It's not like it's a lifetime scar," I said.

Maris and I sat side by side in chairs at the piercing parlor at the boardwalk. The Linleys were taking a family trip and had invited Alex, Maris, Peter and I to come. Ricky was not amused to lose all of us for five days.

"Is it going to hurt?" Maris asked the man preparing her belly button. "Jace, you get your belly button pierced too."

I laughed. I had already gone through my piercing experience and had a small stud in the side of my nose.

My sister pointed at me. "She's getting her belly button done too. I'm paying!"

I looked at Peter, who started laughing. "Fine. But Peter is getting it done too!"

Peter's jaw dropped, then laughed.

It was awesome being at the beach. Our fake IDs weren't believable, but no one seemed to care when it came to taking our money. Mom was going to love this kind of trouble. Afterall, it was the kind of irresponsibility she had been hoping for us to experience.

epilogue 2

"What is this?" I asked as Ky led me deeper into the Campus Winter Wonderland. It had snowed for three days straight, and classes had been canceled. We were a few days from finals and planned to go home for Winter Break. We were happy and in a very healthy two year relationship. We made sure we each had our own friends to go out with, and we didn't live in one another's pockets.

Ky twirled me around and stopped me in place, ignoring my question. "You're so beautiful it hurts my heart, Jace."

I smiled. "I think it was probably the cafeteria fare that did that."

"No. I want you to know something." He wrapped his arms around me and buried his face in my neck, kissing a line up to my ear, so he could whisper, "I loved you like a boy does a girl in tenth grade. But I love you like a man does a woman now."

I swallowed and felt my lashes dampen. He'd never said those words. He'd come close in so many non verbal ways, but never committed those words until now.

"I love you too." I kissed his lips. His cold nose touched mine.

"Good, because there comes a time in every girl's life when she asks herself, are you a dorm kind of girl, or are you an apartment kind of girl?"

"What do you mean?" I asked.

He launched off with, "We have studios, one bedroom or two bedrooms... And then there is the apartment, town-house, or condo?"

"Wait, Ky! Really?" I gasped. "Do they allow cats, dogs, or fish?"

"I do have a thing for Swedish Fish." He kissed my brow.

"I'm all in."

just so you know (jsyk)

You can actually play Pokémon Go with Taylor (TayinNSlayin) by friending him with his Trainer Code. Just add the code below to receive gifts and play along.

Trainer Code: 4396 6161 7952

acknowledgments

I want to thank Bri Lind for all her work in my books and for putting commas in the right places. I have no idea how to use them.

I love you, Chanel Johnson; you are The Queen of Ali Land and Kalie Gerwig for being the wind beneath my everything else.

Creative Paramita designed the cover of It Feels Like Home.

My Beta Beauties: Raylene, Diana, and Erin... Muchas gracias, amigas. It Feels Like Home was so hard to mold because the tense I chose to write it in was balls.

My ARC team and those who leave reviews. I can't thank you enough! Please don't stop. My ego needs more love.

Xpresso Tours for their incredible support and professionalism. Giselle is a rockstar.

Stay-Sea, my soul sister, PoGo Wednesday friend, and fellow vegan food monster. I can't wait for our North West Tour.

The Pizza Guy who gives me an endless supply of coffee, love, and burritos. Thank you for allowing me this indulgence despite the sink on our bank account.

Bean, who is my biggest fan.

My six kitters: Zed, Ms. Peepers, Mr. Wigglesworth, Lovey Dovey, Nala Lala Lily Way, and Mitzy of Meowington. Thanks for all the kitty therapy; the drama isn't necessary—let's cut that out.

about the author

Clare Lukas is the pen name of Ali Lucia Sky, a rather weird and reclusive travel-lover from Northeastern Pennsylvania. She loves to play Pokemón Go, eat vegan food, and watch football and hockey. She is reading or writing when not playing games, eating, or watching sports–so you may find her in bookstores or book conventions. She'd love to see you at a book signing.

Email: authorclarelukas@gmail.com

Website: https://AuthorClareLukas.com

Facebook: https://www.facebook.com/
AuthorClareLukas

also by clare lukas

Young Adult/Teen Romance

It Feels Like Home

The kindest way to thank an author for a good read is with a review.

Please take a moment to leave your thoughts on Amazon, Bookbub, or Goodreads. That would be incredible. I always love to hear from readers; if you want to share anything with me, feel free to contact me at authorclarelukas@gmail.com.

That includes any errors you've found in my novel…